Hillel Halkin

Melisande!
What Are Dreams?

GRANTA

Granta Publications, 12 Addison Avenue, London W11 4QR

First published in Great Britain by Granta Books 2012
Paperback edition published by Granta Books 2013

A CIP catalogue record for this book
is available from the British Library.

1 3 5 7 9 10 8 6 4 2

ISBN 978 1 84708 500 9

Typeset by M Rules
Printed and bound by CPI Group (UK) Ltd, Croydon, CR0 4YY

When he spotted me at a café table in Madrid airport, I hadn't seen Jerome Spector since our high school graduation. He was on his way to Singapore in a three-piece suit and gold-rimmed glasses, and he was the same cheerful bore I remembered him as.

I was sorry he had recognized me. I was waiting for an evening flight to Málaga while working on a talk I had to give at a conference there the next morning; unless I finished it now, I'd have to get up early to do it in my hotel room. But Spector had time before his flight, too, and he wanted me to know how well life had treated him since graduation day. A senior partner in a New York law firm specializing in corporate acquisitions, he was traveling to negotiate the purchase of a Singaporean heavy-lift shipping company by a U.S.–Spanish consortium.

By the time we parted, I knew a lot about heavy-lift ships; also, about Spector's law career, two marriages, several children, and opinions on the U.S. trade deficit. In return, I explained that my talk had to do with a book, *The Incoherence of The Philosophers*, written by an eleventh-century Muslim thinker named Abu Hamid al-Ghazali.

"Do you read Arabic?" Spector asked.

"No," I said. "It's been translated. I'm in ancient Greek and early medieval philosophy."

"I always thought you'd be a writer. Didn't you edit the literary magazine in our senior year?"

"Yes," I said.

"With Ricky Silverman and Mellie Milgram, wasn't it?"

"Yes," I said. "The three of us."

"I forget what it was called."

"*Helicon*."

"Right. *Helicon*. Not that I ever knew what that meant."

"It was said to be the mount of the muses."

"I thought that was Parnassus. I suppose you heard about Ricky."

"Yes."

"Dave Dorenson told me years ago. We're still in touch. I always wondered what happened to Mellie. Melisande: that was her real name."

"Was it?"

"She once told me. Did you know that Fred Abrams was elected to the Senate from New Jersey? And we laughed when he ran for school president."

In the end, his flight was called. Why is it that the passengers lined up at a departure gate make me think of the dead waiting to be ferried across the Styx, a boarding pass in their hands instead of a coin beneath their tongues for Charon the boatman?

★

Melisande! Was ist Traum?
Was ist Tod? Nur eitel Töne.
In der Liebe nur ist Wahrheit,
Und dich lieb ich, ewig Schöne.

Do you remember, Mellie? The cabin by the pond, the cold, cold water, our naked bodies warming by the fire?

We watched the sun drop behind the pond. The autumn trees were reflected in it. They grew upside-down, their shimmering trunks descending to their branches. You said:

"It's a fairy world. Do you think there are still nymphs and water sprites down there?"

"It's easy to see why people once believed in them," I said.

"Yes," you said. "They were young and foolish. Now even the water sprites are old and wise. They look up at the reflection of the trees in the sky and they say, 'It's easy to see why we once believed in earthlings.'"

"When we were in high school," I said, "Ricky told me that once, in third or fourth grade, he was looking out the window and suddenly he wondered, how did he know he wasn't dreaming what he saw? Maybe there was no one else beside him and it would all disappear when he woke up."

"And leave not a rack behind," you said.

"I told him I'd had a thought like that, too. Only what I thought was: suppose someone is dreaming me and *he* wakes up."

"Were you scared?" you asked.

"A little," I said. "Wouldn't you have been?"

"Yes," you said. "But I would have been more scared if I had been Ricky."

Do you remember? If we joined all our memories together, would they be the tiniest part of what we've forgotten? If we added what we only think we remember, would it be the tiniest part of the tiniest part?

★

Ricky and I met in the lunchroom at the start of our sophomore year. The large basement space had a low ceiling that dripped with the paper wrappers of drinking straws. Some marksman of yore had discovered that if you opened them at one end, wet the other, and blew into the straw, the wrappers shot up and stuck to the ceiling. Before falling off they were joined by so many others that

3

placing a new one in an available spot was a sport like archery. The custom was tolerated, having acquired the sanctity of tradition.

There was a rumpus at the lunchroom's far end. A crowd had formed around a table. I made my way toward it and heard someone say, "Syngman Rhee is a fucking fascist, man! He started the war."

"The hell he did."

"It's a fact."

"In *The Daily Jerkoff*."

"A better paper than your *Times*. All the news that's shit in print."

I pushed my way into the crowd to get a look at the boy at the table. He had pale skin, a fine nose, and full, dark hair, and he seemed to relish being one against many. "So how do you explain," he was asked, "that the South Korean army was in full retreat an hour after launching a surprise attack?"

"How do you explain, brother," he said, "that my dog jumped a cat in the park the other day and then turned tail and ran? He ran 'cause that cat clawed him good."

After the crowd had drifted off, I stayed behind. He had an odd stare, one eye coming toward you and the other holding back, like the two fists of a boxer. When I returned it, I saw that the eyes were different colors: the green eye jabbed while the brown eye kept its guard up. He grinned and said:

"I'll bet you think I'm full of shit, too."

"You win your bet," I said.

★

Ricky's dog was named Pinky. He was a little Scotch terrier with so great a fear of abandonment that he had to be shut in the coat closet of the Silvermans' West End Avenue apartment to be kept from defending the front door against anyone departing.

Ricky's parents were active Party members. Ralph Silverman worked as an accountant for the city. Tillie Silverman was a pharmacist. Once or twice a week, they went out at night without saying where. According to Ricky, they had keys to a safe house and kept suitcases packed for a dash to it. That might have been true. Those were the McCarthy years. They could have been jailed on the Smith Act.

It was the autumn of the first Eisenhower–Stevenson campaign. I was a fourteen-year-old anarchist for Stevenson. Timbrous and plangent, his cultivated voice over the airwaves made me shiver.

Ricky laughed at me. "He's just another bourgeois politician," he said. "For a voice, I'll take Perry Como." He pronounced the word "bujwa," as if it were something on a French menu that no honest American could be expected to get right.

Some nights we walked along Broadway, listening to the sound trucks. It was the last election in which they were out in force, charging the chill October air with an electric crackle – the last of the old Greek agora to adhere to the city's streets. Crowds gathered, jacket collars turned up against the cold. The heckling was good-natured. Only once, when Ricky was called a "Commie bastard" for shouting something about the Rosenbergs, did I have to hustle him away.

We didn't talk politics that much. After a while, the same arguments grew boring. We cared more for sports. I was good at them; Ricky was better. He could dribble and shoot with either hand and run straight at you with a football and swivel past you without a finger being laid on him. Although he mostly ignored the school coaches who begged him to come to try-outs, he did turn out on a dare one spring for baseball practice. He hit a double and a triple, threw out a runner from right field, and walked away with a wave of his hand when offered a place on the starting line-up.

There was a bunch of us West Siders: Danny Shapiro, Ben Hyman, Henry Taub, Eddie Bronstein, Ricky, and me. We'd take a basketball to Riverside Park and find an empty court, or challenge for one if none was free. If you won, it was yours until you lost. You didn't argue with the other team over who did what. It was adults – referees, umpires, authority of any kind – who made you cheat or play dirty. Without them, if a ball went out-of-bounds and you said it didn't, or you fouled someone and denied it, there would be a fight and the game would break up. You had to be fair. We all knew it would be a better world without grown-ups.

In one of these games, I saw Ricky outplay a boy from George Washington high who made the city all-stars that year. Nothing fazed him except the pigeons. The park was full of them. Old people sat on benches and scattered breadcrumbs, and the birds, who were fatter than the people, gathered to squabble over the crumbs. They were so dumb that if a crumb fell from their beaks, they forgot all about it and went to look for another. Some artistes trained them to eat from their hands and perch on them as if roosting in trees. Ricky called them the crumb-bums and gave them a wide berth.

Once a pigeon flew at him from a crumb-bum's shoulder and he panicked. He threw a ball at it, and when that missed, pulled his shirt over his head and screamed.

"They'll peck your fucking eyes out," he said when it flew off.

"Where'd you get that from?" I said. "You're thinking of crows."

"I'm thinking of pigeons," he said. "They'll do what the crumb-bums tell them to."

Sometimes we shot pool or bowled in an alley on Broadway,

where we set pins for fifty cents an hour and a free game for every ten we worked. In the pit behind the pins, unseen by the bowlers, you felt like a puppeteer until a ball rumbling toward you made it more like dodging missiles from a catapult.

Once, on our way home, we stopped to eat at a Horn & Hardart's. They're gone now, those old automats. You plunked down a dollar at the cashier's, scooped up an avalanche of nickels and dimes that shot out as though from a slot machine, and fed them into little windows with sandwiches and pies and things.

A boy stood crying by the ham sandwich window. He was ten or eleven, with a soiled New York Giants hat on his head and a runny nose that had clotted into a yellow resin.

"What's the matter?" Ricky asked.

"I put in four nickels and didn't get no sandwich," the boy said.

The window said 25 CENTS.

"Put in another," I told him.

"That's all I had."

I reached into my pocket for a nickel. Ricky said, "Let's have your hat, kid."

The boy looked at him fearfully

"Come on, hand it over."

He gave Ricky his Giants hat and Ricky filled it with a dollar's worth of change and gave it back. "Let's get out of here," he said as if we were a gang of shoplifters.

★

Long before the Twentieth Party Congress, Ricky's parents got wind of something. They exchanged sharp, coded remarks.

"You shouldn't have attacked him like that."

"He's a Trot, Ralph."

"He's no Trot, for God's sake. I don't know what makes you

say that. He's just asking you to face up to what happened. There were mistakes."

"That's immaterial. Mistakes are made by people, not by history."

You could see Ricky struggling. I could take a dig now at the Soviet Union without provoking his automatic scorn. He even surprised me by saying, "You know, maybe Trotsky had it right."

"How's that?" I asked.

"He said the dictatorship of the proletariat had become a dictatorship of the Party bureaucracy. That another revolution was needed for the workers to take back power."

We were in our junior year. We had both signed up for Caroline Ames' creative writing class. One of the first exercises she gave us was to write a short description of the student sitting next to us. I sat next to Joanna Steiglitz and my description began:

"Her earrings give me motion sickness. She says they come from Mexico, but who knows where her smile's from?"

Joanna's long silver earrings came from Fred Leighton's on MacDougal Street. We'd take the D train down to Washington Square after school – Joanna, Ricky, Julie Rappaport, Peter Spatz, Peter Alcalay, Andy Galton – and sit in the Figaro or the Rienzi, drinking espresso and smoking and pretending we were in Paris. Sometimes, if someone's parents were away, we'd get together at their apartment. Peter Alcalay would bring his guitar and we'd sit on the floor with a gallon of wine and paper cups and sing "Green Sleeves" and "Careless Love" and "Down In The Valley" and "Take This Hammer" and "All My Trials" and "If I Had Wings Like Noah's Dove," and then "Passing Through" and "Joe Hill" and "Union Miner" and "Greenback Dollar" and "The Banks Are Made of Marble" and "*Viva La Quince Brigada*" and "*Los Quatro Generales*" and "Peatbog Soldiers" until we were all

8

stretched out on our backs, my head in Joanna's lap and Joanna's in Julie's and Julie's in Peter Spatz's, and Peter Alcalay would switch to the blues. He was good. Years later he cut a record on some small label.

There was a Saturday night like that, after the last guitar chords had faded into a dreamy silence, when someone put on a Bill Haley record and we jitterbugged. You and I danced together. It was hard to keep up with you. No one else moved like that. Ricky stood watching. For all his natural coordination, he didn't like to dance. After a while, he pulled me away and steered me to the kitchen.

"I've been reading this book by Albert Caymiss," he said.

"What book?"

"*The Rebel.* There's this part about Sisyphus. You know, the guy in Greek mythology who has to push a stone up a hill. Every time he gets it almost to the top, it rolls back down and he has to start all over."

"Yeah?" I wanted to get back to you.

"Caymiss says the Revolution is like that. In the end, it always crushes you. The rebel is the one who won't give up. He keeps pushing the stone up the hill again, even though he knows it's absurd. The question is, is he a schmuck or not."

Camus was just the beginning. Ricky threw himself into books as if sure of finding the answer there. I followed, not wanting to be left behind. We emptied the shelves of the Bloomingdale branch of the public library on 100th Street like shoppers at a clearance sale. There was no rhyme or reason to any of it. We read Plato, and Hermann Hesse, and *The Magic Mountain*, and *Portrait of the Artist*, and *Thus Spake Zarathustra*, swallowing all we could get down. I started Kierkegaard's *The Sickness Unto Death* because it was mentioned as "seminal," a word I had to look up, in a paperback on existentialism I had bought at a second-hand stand and gave up after the first sentence. I read *Look Homeward, Angel* in three days, cutting school to do it. I read Alberto Moravia's *Bread and Wine*, and Sartre's *Nausea*, and D.H. Lawrence's *Sons and Lovers*.

Ricky showed up in Mr. Tyson's chemistry class with *Crime and Punishment*. He didn't glance up from it when asked for the formula of carbonic acid. "Richard. Silverman," said Mr. Tyson, "you would do us a great favor by putting away that book and paying attention." "I'm sorry," Ricky said, still reading, "but it says here that all things are permitted if God does not exist." He was thrown out of class and nearly suspended.

That launched his Dostoyevsky period. "Jesus," he said to me. "I wake up in the morning not knowing if I'm Prince Mishkin or Peter Verezhovensky." We were sprawled on the bed in his bedroom. "There's a place where Ivan says to Alyosha. . .just a minute, let me find it. . .here, where he says: 'Imagine that you are creating a fabric of human destiny with the object of making men happy in the end, giving them peace and rest at last, but that it was essential and inevitable to torture to death only one tiny creature – a baby beating its breast with its fist, for example – and to found that edifice on its unavenged tears, would you consent to be the architect on those conditions? Tell me, and tell the truth.'"

"I can't," I said. "I mean I can't imagine what edifice could be founded on the death of a baby."

"I wasn't asking you. Ivan asks Alyosha. And Alyosha says, 'No, I wouldn't consent.' And Ivan asks again, 'And can you admit the idea that the men for whom you are building it would agree to accept their happiness on the foundation of the unexpiated blood of a little victim?'"

"What does Alyosha say to that?"

"He says that killing the baby would be unforgivable. That only God could forgive such a thing."

"Then babies have a bright future."

"Then Raskolnikov is wrong."

"Why?"

"Because if Alyosha is right, all things could be permitted only if God did exist."

"Even if he did, that wouldn't solve my problem."

"What's that?"

"It's not the baby's death," I said. "It's mine."

I didn't want to die, ever. I wanted to watch a million suns set, love a million women, walk down a million city streets and lonely roads. A thousand lifetimes wouldn't be enough for that. Sometimes, convinced I had come down with some fatal illness, I was afraid I wouldn't even have one.

There was a boy in school named Marvin Wolfowitz who wore a skullcap and had the reputation of being a scientific genius. Passing him one day in the luchroom as he was whispering to himself, Ricky inquired, "Hey, Rabbi, what's all the mumbo-jumbo?"

Marvin Wolfowitz signaled Ricky to wait until he was done and then replied with the equanimity of those who have seen their persecutors come and go:

"It was a prayer of thanks for the food I ate."

"Ah. Then would it be fair to assume you believe there is a God in this world who listens to your prayers, Mr. Wolfowitz?" asked Ricky in a voice like Mr. Tyson's.

"No," Marvin Wolfowitz said.

"No?"

"The world is in God, not God in the world, even though the formal properties of any set are fully present in all its subsets."

"Then where the fuck is he?" Ricky asked.

"Who?"

"God."

"Everywhere."

"Where?"

"Here." Marvin Wolfowitz stuck out a hand and snapped it shut as if trapping a fly.

"In your *fist*?"

"Yes."

I had never seen Ricky so unsure of himself. He turned to me for help, but I was staring at Marvin Wolfowitz's fist. It was white and pudgy, with a raw cuticle at the base of the thumb.

"All right, Wolfowitz," Ricky said. "Open it."

"Why should I?"

"Because if you don't, I'll make you."

"Try."

Ricky seized Marvin Wolfowitz's fist and tried prying it open. Wolfowitz resisted with surprising strength. Each time a new finger was forced up, an old one slid craftily shut again. Ricky was flushed from exertion. The green-eyed side of his face was redder than the brown-eyed side. In the end, he opened Wolfowitz's fist. There were sweaty ink stains on the palm.

★

How might I have described you, Mellie, had you sat next to me instead of next to Jerome Spector? I might have written:

"Watching her, I ask: is she the bird or the branch it is sitting on?"

★

It was Spector who started that argument over your poem. I'd forgotten it until I came across it in an old issue of *Helicon* that I

12

found at the bottom of a carton. Caroline Ames handed us mimeographed copies and read it aloud.

> The world, reflected in a tinkling edge of glass,
> Becomes as one, a whirling, toiling mass
> Of faces known and faces strange
> And faces loved and hated in the past,
> Of those I knew were friends, and true,
> And those that failed me in my quest.
> They merge and form again anew.
>
> Why does your face stand out above the rest?

"Comments, anyone?" Caroline Ames asked.

"It's beautiful, Mellie," Julie Rappaport said.

Most of the class agreed. Someone praised your having made the last line stand alone, giving it the weight of all the other lines. Someone pointed out that the only unrhymed end-word was "strange," which made it a stranger in the poem.

That was when Spector raised his hand. "I hate to be a party pooper," he said, "but Mellie's rhyme scheme isn't consistent. She has 'glass,' 'mass,' 'strange,' and 'past' – that's AABA – and then 'true,' 'quest,' 'anew,' and 'rest' – that's CDCD."

"Jesus, Spector," Ricky said. "It's a poem, not a quadratic equation."

"Poetry has rules just like algebra," Spector retorted.

Someone countered with the example of free verse. Someone said "past" rhymed as much with "quest" and "rest" as it did with "glass" and "mass." Someone said it didn't.

Caroline Ames wrote "assonance" and "consonance" on the blackboard. Peter Spatz passed me a note that said:

"Is Jerome Spector an assonance or a cuntsonance?"

And all that while you listened intently, turning your head toward whoever spoke. When there were no more hands in the air, Caroline Ames asked:

"Would you like to say anything, Mellie?"

You shook your head.

"Anyone else?"

There was no one. I hadn't said a word. What should I have said – that I wished that face were mine?

★

Toward the end of the year, Caroline Ames invited the three of us to the *Helicon* office and asked us to be the magazine's next editors. "You're my best writers," she said. "I'm sure you'll work well together."

We went out for Chinese food to celebrate. You tried teaching me to use chopsticks. I dropped a piece of Sechuan pork in my tea and asked for a fork.

We discussed our plans for *Helicon*. You wanted to sponsor fiction and poetry contests to encourage new contributors. We would publish the winners and give them prizes.

Ricky thought there was enough fiction and poetry already. He was for serious essays. "Read the last issue," he said. "It's all first kisses and raindrops on windows and little old ladies on benches who once were young. We need hard truths, not beautiful feelings."

"Beauty is truth," I said.

"Bullshit! Keats was just playing with words. What's true about a beautiful woman or beautiful about Stalin's murdering the kulaks?"

"It's not the woman or the kulaks. It's the laws of aesthetics

14

and the rules of evidence. They're about the same things: harmony, parsimony, non-contradiction."

"The rules of evidence explain why Mellie is so sexy?"

"Of course they do. Don't you think so, Mellie?"

"I think you're both talking hoo-ha," you said. "I just don't know who's hoo and who's ha."

"Try *Who's Hoo In America*," I suggested.

"Most likely," you said, "Hoo is you."

I was Hoo for you from then on.

★

That crazy trip to Philadelphia!

We went by bus because it was cheaper than train. There was a workshop of high school literary magazine editors on the University of Pennsylvania campus, from which all the students were gone because it was the start of the Christmas vacation.

The workshop ended on the afternoon of the second day and there was transportation back to the Greyhound terminal that we didn't take because you suddenly remembered you had an aunt in Chestnut Hill and couldn't leave Philadelphia without seeing her. "We'll just pop in and pop out," you said. But the taxi let us off on the wrong street, and we had to walk a mile in the cold, and it was dark when we got there, and you and your Aunt Trude talked on and on in French (you had never told us you were born in Belgium), and she insisted we stay for dinner, which meant waiting for your uncle to come home. There was nothing to worry about, you said, because they would drive us to the terminal and the last bus for New York left at ten-twenty. But it had begun to snow, and your uncle decided to put chains on his tires and took a long time doing it, and we reached the terminal at ten-fifteen – which still would have been all right if

15

you hadn't gotten it backwards and the last bus hadn't left at twenty-to.

Your aunt and uncle had driven off. We couldn't ask them to come back for us in a snowstorm. You called home from a pay phone, told your mother we were spending another night on the Penn campus, and asked her to let Ricky's and my parents know.

We went to look at the departures board. The next bus to New York was at six in the morning. A bus was about to leave for San Francisco.

"I say we take it," Ricky said.

For a moment, it almost seemed possible.

The San Francisco bus pulled out. The snack bar shut down. The terminal was empty except for the derelicts who drifted into such places at night – the bums, the winos, the queers looking for a pick-up. We looked like three runaways ourselves.

A man and two women came in from the street. The man handed each woman a small package and they went to the ladies' room.

"He's their pimp," Ricky said. "They're going to shoot up."

You were afraid to go to the ladies' room by yourself and asked us to stand guard by the door. Then someone threw up on a bench. We went to look for some coffee. The snow turned to ice water in our shoes. We found a diner with a single customer who had fallen asleep with his face in a plate of hash-browns. We slipped out of our shoes beneath the counter, peeled off our wet socks with our toes, and sat there until closing time. Then we walked back to the terminal and chose a corner to lie down in. We made pillows of our jackets and lay in a row with you in the middle.

"Mellie," I said, "tell us a bedtime story."

"About what?" you asked.

"About anything."

You told a story about a princess and a moth. The princess lived in a castle with many servants. Whenever she was hungry, they brought her favorite foods. Each time she grew bored, they had a new game to play. She had only to yawn and a palanquin appeared.

"What's a palanquin?" I asked.

"It's a bed carried on shoulders," you said.

The princess was tired of all this. For hours she sat looking out the window of her room. She saw the castle's turrets, and beyond them, the moat, and beyond that, fields and mountains and towns. Although she wanted to explore it all, she knew that her parents, the king and queen, would never let her cross the moat until she married a prince who took her to another castle.

The princess decided to run away. She was frightened. How would she manage on her own? Where would she find food and shelter?

One night, a big gray moth came to her bedside while she slept. It fluttered its wings on the night table and said:

"If you want to leave the castle, I'll give you a ring with a stone so rare that it's the only one of its kind. It will protect you."

"A magic ring!" the princess exclaimed.

"Oh, no," the moth said. "This ring can't do any tricks."

"Then how will it protect me?" she asked.

"Everyone," the moth said, "will want to buy it from you. You'll be offered a great price."

"Then I'll sell it," the princess said, "and have all the money I need."

"I wouldn't do that if I were you," said the moth.

"Why not?" asked the princess.

"Sell it and you'll see," the moth said.

When she awoke early in the morning, the princess found a

ring on the table. She slipped it onto her finger, stepped into the dark hallway, and stood outside her sleeping parents' room. Then she tiptoed down the castle stairs, slid open the bolt on the heavy door, found the guard fast asleep by the drawbridge, turned the wheel that lowered it, and crossed the moat.

"Go on," I said. You had stopped.

"I can't," you said.

"Why not?"

"Because I don't know what happens next."

"Did she sell the ring?" Ricky asked.

You didn't answer. I opened my eyes to look at you. There was a single tear on your cheek.

*

I was heading downstairs between classes when someone called:

"Arjuna!"

It was Ricky. He was standing on the landing above me.

"Hey, Arjuna, I found it!"

Arms spread wide, he declaimed:

"Your words are wise, Arjuna, but your sorrow is for nothing. The truly wise mourn neither for the living nor for the dead.

"There was never a time when I did not exist, nor you, nor any of these kings. Nor is there any future in which we shall cease to be.

"Just as the dweller in this body passes through childhood, youth, and old age, so at death he passes into another body. The wise are not deceived by that."

He paid no attention to the students and teachers staring at him.

"That's not good enough," I shouted back.

*

Fucking Ricky!

"Oh, come on, Hoo," you said. "He'll be back in a week."

"If it's a week in which Ralph and Tillie keep calling me every night, I won't survive it," I said.

They were frantic. Ricky had left them a note saying he was heading out west and they would hear from him.

On a pad in the *Helicon* office he had written:

"And then Tom he talked along, and talked along, and says, let's all three slide out of here, one of these nights, and go for howling adventures among the Injuns, over in the Territory, for a couple of weeks or so; and I say, all right, that suits me. But I reckon I got to light out for the Territory ahead of the rest."

"He's probably rafting down the Mississippi right now," I said.

"I hope not," you said. "There are floods there. I saw it on TV. He'll end up stranded on top of some levee and we'll have to go with a ladder to get him down."

My chagrin at his not having asked me to join him was only aggravated by my relief that he hadn't. But I did like having you to myself. Our spring issue was due out in a month and we were still missing half of it. We hadn't read the entries in the short story contest and the essay Ricky had planned to call "Cop-Out In The Rye" could be forgotten.

We worked hard, you harder than me because you didn't sit there watching me all the time. When you concentrated, the tip of your tongue slipped through your lips as if you were about to wet a thread for a needle. You wrote me notes in a neat, looping hand in the margins of the stories, the jade ring I had bought you at Fred Leighton's on your finger. You wrote: "It would work better without this passage." "Don't bother with this one. It's plagiarized from *True Romance* comics." "Do you think he really slept with her?"

"No," I wrote back. "But don't make him lie to you by asking."

Although few of them would have admitted it, most of the boys I knew were virgins. Or were until, while Ricky was away, our West Side gang went to a prostitute. Eddie Bronstein had gotten her number and negotiated for a group rate. She was known as Black Lily and I took some razzing for saying I wasn't going to a whore named like a horse.

They came to school the next day grinning and whooping like a party of braves back from a scalping raid. Only Eddie kept apart from it. "So honestly," I asked him. "How was it?"

"Honestly? Honestly, jerking off is better," Eddie said.

None of the stories was very good. First prize was two tickets to *Waiting For Godot* and we decided to award it to ourselves. It was the première Broadway production with Bert Lahr. Afterwards, we sat in a cafeteria on 57th Street, arguing what it was about.

We went together to the Museum of Modern Art. You stood for a long time in front of Van Gogh's *The Starry Night*. "He's something, isn't he?" I said.

"The town is asleep," you said. "It doesn't know the sky above it has gone mad. The cypress tree is praying for them both."

★

Ricky came back two months later. He had gotten as far as Wyoming, hitching most of the way. He had baled hay on a ranch near Cheyenne and learned to drive a tractor, and he had stories to tell about highways and truck stops and four-dollar-a-night motels and places where the bathrooms said "White" and "Colored" and elderly Negroes called you "boss" and stepped off the sidewalk to let you pass. In Laconia, Tennessee he decided to step off it first. The black man coming toward him was so rattled that he stopped in his tracks. A car pulled up and the driver asked Ricky where he was from. "New York," he said. "Is that so?" said the driver. "Then get your Yankee ass back there before I smoke it and hang it from a rafter."

In Arkansas, he was arrested for vagrancy. He and a policeman watched television and played two-handed canasta. He was locked in a cell for the night and let go with a fine the next day.

In east Missouri, a woman gave him a lift, brought him home, emptied his knapsack into her washing machine, and took him to bed with her. In the morning she folded his clean clothes, made him toast and coffee, packed him a lunch, and told him to leave by the back door and walk three blocks to a traffic light where he could pick up Route 30 going west.

It wasn't like Black Lily. "That was real pussy," Ricky said.

Later that day, he caught a ride all the way to Cheyenne. It was a strange experience. "The guy was a shoe salesman. He had to be in Cheyenne in the morning. That meant driving all night. I told him I didn't have a license and he said, 'Never mind, I'll do the driving. I just need to stay awake. I don't want to have to make conversation, so don't talk to me. You're in charge of the radio. Make sure there's something on it all the time. I don't care if it's Jesus-loves-you or cream-of-wheat, but I'll fall asleep without it.'

"The car's got this punch-button radio. It's corn country. There aren't many stations on the air in the middle of the night. The salesman's doing eighty and I'm punching buttons like mad because I'm afraid he'll kill us if I stop. I get some country music from Omaha, and then there's static, so I switch to a talk show, and after that there's a preacher and Chuck Berry singing 'Earth Angel,' except someone else is talking about a Pontiac sale in

Boulder and someone else about thunderstorms in the Rockies. Then I lose them both and the next thing I hear is, 'This is WZBT in Spokane, Washington,' and how the hell can it be Spokane when that's a thousand miles away and I can't get Omaha?

"We're the only car on the road. The whole fucking country is talking in its sleep, he died for your sins, and will you be mine, and ten percent off, and dropping into the forties, and no one is listening except me and this crazy salesman who shuts one eye at a time and keeps the other open with a finger. I say, 'Why don't you pull over and get some sleep,' and he says, 'You promised not to talk,' and I don't want him letting me off in a cornfield, so I punch another button. In the end we both must have nodded off, because I suddenly woke and the car was skidding all over the road. I knew I was going to die – I mean it was obvious – and that's when this weird thing happened. It just didn't happen to me because I wasn't me any more. I'd like burst open and flowed over everything. I was still in the car, but I was the car too, and the road it was skidding on, and I didn't care if it went off it because I was the tree it would smash into and the ditch it would land up in. It only lasted a couple of seconds. We spun around twice and ended up facing in the same direction we'd been driving in. That son-of-a-bitch didn't pull over even then. He just said 'Fucking shit!' and kept on driving."

Ricky stayed a day in Cheyenne and hit Route 30 again. A rancher in a pick-up truck gave him a ride and offered him work. He spent six weeks on the ranch and took a Greyhound back to New York.

He was suntanned. Ralph and Tillie were thrilled to have him home. They didn't have long to celebrate, though, because the next day he told them he wasn't going back to school. They begged him to change his mind. It was only the first week of

June. He had done well on his College Boards, had gotten into Cornell with a state scholarship, and could still cram for the Regents and graduate with the rest of us. He refused. "It's pathetic," he said to me after a fight at home. "They raised me on Big Bill Haywood and the Wobblies, and now they're hysterical because I won't be walking around an Ivy League campus in a corduroy jacket."

He was thinking of going west again or shipping out on a freighter. He had decided to live like a bhikshu.

"A what?"

"That's a bum, Arjuna. The bhikshu is satisfied with sufficient robes to cover his body, with sufficient food to fill his stomach. Whithersoever he may go forth, these he takes with him as he goes — just as a bird with its wings, withersoever it may fly, carries its wings with it as it flies. Thus it is that the bhikshu is content."

"And how does the bhikshu stay content withersoever his food runs out?" I asked.

"He begs. At least that's the classical conception. I'm not sure it will wash in these United States. I may have to cheat by working. The important thing is to keep moving. A bhikshu develops an attachment to no place."

A bhikshu also had no savings. Apart from what was left from his ranch earnings, Ricky still had some of his bowling money. Altogether, it came to slightly more than three hundred dollars. It was surprising how hard it was to get rid of it the way he wanted, by handing it out in Central Park.

I went with him reluctantly. It didn't strike me as a bright idea and his attempt to explain it didn't make it more so. "Sure, I could donate it to some charity," he said. "But that's not the same as giving it away to strangers bit by bit. That's like taking the. . .oh, fuck it, man, let's go."

23

What it was like was a first fling at begging. Of the dozens of people we approached that day, most refused to take Ricky's money and many of the takers had to be cajoled. "I beg your pardon!" huffed a lady as we set out on the cinder path around the reservoir at the north end of the park. Further along it, a black woman wheeling a white baby in a carriage scolded, "You take that money and give it back to your mama or who you stole it from!" She looked at me accusingly. "You get this boy home before he get into real trouble, you hear?"

It was unpredictable. Crossing the baseball diamonds south of 86th Street, Ricky held out a bill to a sanitation worker spearing litter. "Excuse me, sir," he said. "I'm giving out money today."

As the man stepped back in alarm, raising his pronged stick like a startled hunter, a suited gentleman came by and said:

"If you don't mind, I'll take that."

He plucked the bill from Ricky's hand like a napkin from its holder.

A drunk slumped against a tree quickly pocketed his share as if fearing to wake from a dream. A man reading a newspaper tossed his away without looking, thinking it a commercial flyer. A woman in a silk blouse and cravate whispered to me as Ricky handed a dollar apiece to two giggling girls on roller skates:

"Don't let that person out of your sight, young man. I'm going to call the police."

There had been a thunderstorm the day before and it was one of those New York summer days that sent the squirrels scampering down from the trees for a better look at the blue frosting of the sky. We worked our way southwards, buying vanilla pops from a Good Humor man whom Ricky told to keep the change. On the bridge over the lake, we stood watching the rowers pass beneath us. Ricky made a paper airplane out of a dollar bill and aimed it at a boat. It missed and floated on the scummy green water.

On the mall beyond Bethesda Terrace, a blond bicycle rider braked to let us pass. Ricky offered him five dollars. The rider said:

"Twenty is my minimum."

Ricky peeled off another five and a ten and he rode off.

Some people thought it was an advertising stunt and looked for a hidden camera. Others were curious. Ricky told a man in sunglasses that he was out to win a bet and a woman with a gold cross around her neck that he had been assigned a penance by his priest. At the carousel, he informed a mother lifting her son onto a painted horse that he had two months left to live. "That's if I'm lucky. Everyone says I should take the money and enjoy it, but I'd rather do some good before I die."

It took all morning. "That's it," he said after tying his next-to-last bill to the string of a helium balloon and letting it rise over the zoo near 59th Street. "I've got five bucks left. I'll treat you to a taxi."

The ride home cost two dollars thirty. He tipped the cabbie seventy cents and handed me what was left. "For your pains, Arjuna," he said.

★

Ricky didn't come to our graduation. When it was over, we sent our parents home with our diplomas and hung around for a while outside the school building. Then a bunch of us went for pizza and went on sitting around the table when it was finished, picking at smaller and smaller crusts on the tabletop. We talked about getting together at the summer's end and no one said what we all knew. Catullus knew it, eager to be off:

iam mens praetrepidans avet vagari,
iam laeti studio pedes vigescunt.
o dulces comitum valete coetus,
longe quos simul a domo profectos
diversae varie viae reportant.

That summer my parents traveled to Europe. I saw them off on the *Queen Elizabeth* and had our big apartment to myself. I'd wake up late and lie in bed watching the sunshine filter through the Venetian blinds and then dress and go outside into a great shout of light and heat and have a cruller or a Danish in a luncheonette with my coffee while reading the morning paper, feeling like a tourist in a foreign city I had been in so many times that I didn't have to go anywhere. It was a summer for doing nothing while waiting for everything, which would happen in those mysterious places called Amherst and Swarthmore and Oberlin and Bard that we would depart for in the fall. Yet even as we squandered the time we were tycoons of, we felt a first twinge of the miser's fear that no sum is too large to fritter away.

A few times we went to the beach. You, Joanna, and Julie carried your things in canvas tote bags and Ricky, Peter Alcalay, and I rolled ours in towels and rode the train to Brighton Beach or Coney Island like a party of pilgrims with its prayer rugs. We changed in the locker rooms, and lay in the sand talking and reading, and dived into the waves to cool off. I had never seen you in a bathing suit. I tried keeping my eyes away from the place where your thighs, which still had a thin roll of baby fat, came together. Once a wave threw you against me. You smelled of salt and suntan lotion, and I felt my prick stiffen and let go of you. Afterwards, my balls ached for a long time.

We went to a concert at Lewisohn Stadium. The orchestra played Beethoven's Fifth. The planes flew low overhead on their way to LaGuardia and Idlewild, drowning out the music while the audience lit cigarettes and changed position on the hard stone benches. The cigarettes glowed in the dark night. Long afterwards, thinking of those of us I never saw again – Jo Steiglitz, Julie, Andy Galton – I imagined us all in the same dark universe in which we only had to glow to be seen.

*

In August I went biking in Nova Scotia with Peter Alcalay. We took a ferry from Bar Harbor to Yarmouth, rented bikes, and rode up along the Bay of Fundy.

Ricky was still in the city. He was waiting for an able seaman's ticket promised him by a friend of his father's in the National Maritime Union, and he asked me if he could use my family's apartment while I was away. He had met a girl, he said, and needed a place to be with her.

I gave him the key and told him to drop it off at the super's when he left.

He didn't bother to clean up. My parents' bed was unmade when I returned. There were crumbs on the kitchen table and unwashed dishes in the sink. A fallen note lay on the floor beneath the table.

I must own a fairly complete set of your notes. Now and then they turn up in the pages of the books I stuck them in. Last week one tumbled out of my Archer-Hind edition of the *Phaedo*. It said:

Don't forget:
tomatoes
iceberg lettuce
cukes (no fatties!)
1½ lb. ground chuck
2 eggplants
parmajohn
2 bottles of Mateus
wash at laundromat

That laundromat on Columbus Avenue! You once said that all those clothes going round in the foam made you think of a ship-wreck. That it was like looking through a porthole at drowning passengers in a stormy sea.

You thought fat cucumbers were mealy. I said they tasted just as good and that it took less time to peel one fat one than two thin ones.

We must have had guests for dinner. Who? Moysh and Linda? Eve Trager and that boyfriend of hers who went to South America to study howler monkeys? What day was it? What year? I looked at the paper, the faded ink. I tried remembering why I was reading the *Phaedo*.

It's always like that. I open a book and you're there, reminding me to take out the garbage or pick up my shoes at the shoemaker's, and I wonder when it was and put you back until the next time, when you still won't have learned to spell parme-san.

But that note I found when I came back from Nova Scotia I threw away. I recognized the looping handwriting at once. "Went for fresh rolls," it said. "Be right back."

2

During my years in Cambridge, I tried putting you both out of my mind. Sometimes I succeeded. It was like an ache you think is gone. You're relieved it's not there any more. There's no need to see a doctor after all. And then, just when you've forgotten it, it's back.

I lost all track of you. Once, in New York for the weekend, I met Ralph Silverman coming out of the subway. To be polite, I asked about Ricky. Ralph said he was living "abroad" and I let it go at that.

You called the first time you came home for Thanksgiving from the University of Chicago. I was cold to you on the phone. You didn't call again.

College was a letdown. I suppose Harvard was as good a school as we who were told we were privileged to be its students believed it was. But only once can you make the discovery that there is a world of ideas as real as the ordinary world, and though I saw many of my classmates make it, I had made it long before. There wasn't a lecture in Boylston or Emerson Hall that left me restless with excitement as some of my conversations with Ricky had done.

I majored in Classics. Today I wonder how I had the sense to do that when I was so foolish about so many other things. Even had I gone on to something else, it would have taught me to honor the ancients and spared me the arrogance of the ignorance of them. Yet this wasn't something I thought about as an undergraduate struggling to parse Latin sentences or memorize Greek contract verbs, or later when reading Homer with Cedric Whitman, Ovid with Wendell Clausen, and Philo in a seminar of Harry Wolfson's that I was lucky to take before his retirement. It was that which first interested me in the Neoplatonists.

I lived in Wiggleworth Hall and Dunster House before renting an apartment with a friend on Chester Street. A few months later, Robin moved in with me. She was at Radcliffe; we met when a frisbee she was chasing in the Quad bounced off my back. She was so flustered and pretty that I wouldn't accept an apology unless she agreed to go to the movies with me. A week later, we were sharing a bed.

For a while, it was marvelous. She had a large talent for happiness that made up for my smaller one. It wasn't defeated by me until we started talking about marriage. By then I had been offered a graduate fellowship at Columbia, and for all Robin's desire to come to New York with me − she would get a job in publishing or advertising, we would be able to afford a nice apartment, she was already planning how to furnish it − she wanted it to be as my wife. Although I couldn't conceive of pledging my life to her, I did everything not to admit it. I was determined to prove that the love lacking was hers, that it was she who wasn't prepared for a life with me. The tears I drove her to were as much at the indignity of having to be so angry with me all the time as at the way I behaved. In the end, I got what I wanted: Robin left me and I felt rejected. I graduated summa cum laude and spent the summer in Europe, feeling miserable while getting over her.

*

I dreamed last night that I was in a subway station in New York. It was sleeting and the station smelled like a wet dog. I had to

30

meet you at 96th Street and Central Park West, and there was a long line for tokens, and all the time the turnstiles kept going *push-clunk push-clunk push-clunk*. The cars rumbled on the tracks and I was afraid I'd miss my train. Just then I saw Moysh Muslansky. Melted sleet was dripping from his duffle coat and he held a Goldwater button the size of a shield in one hand. "Moysh, how are you?" I said, and he began telling me about his dissertation on the Wars of the Roses, which still wasn't finished, and all this time the turnstiles kept turning. "But Moysh," I said, hearing my train pull out, "it's been hundreds of years," and he said, "Yes, I'm sorry about Mellie."

It was at that party of his that I saw you and Ricky again.

Moysh gave it to celebrate passing his orals. It was crowded. The music was too loud. I was about to leave when the two of you walked in.

The shock was total. Moysh and Linda had never mentioned you. I hadn't known either of you was in New York. I hadn't known you were together. Whenever I had imagined meeting one of you, rehearsing what I would say, I had never thought of including the other. Now, I wanted only to get to the front door without your seeing me.

Instead, I walked across the room to you, still holding my drink.

You were talking to someone and didn't notice me. Ricky had his back to you. I stood to one side of you, slightly behind you. Your hair was longer, nearly shoulder-length. One more step would take me out of your line of vision.

"Hello, Mellie," I said.

You spun around.

"Hoo!"

"Hoo den?"

31

It had been a gag line of ours.

"I can't believe it's you," you said.

I said, "Don't be so sure of it. I could be an apparition."

You kissed me. "You're definitely corporeal," you said. You pulled Ricky's sleeve. "Rick, look who's here."

He turned to face us. He had gotten broader in the chest.

"Arjuna!" he said. "It's been ages."

"Eons," I said.

He laughed. "Whole *kalpas*. Well! This calls for a toast. What can I get you, Mellie?"

You asked for a scotch on the rocks. Ricky went to get it. The noise was awful. Moysh and Sam Bolowitz were arguing about Cuba. Sam sounded drunk. "We can't talk here," you said. "Get my phone number from Linda and call me, all right?"

"All right," I said. "I'm going. You can toast me in absentia."

I headed for the door. On the way, I was stopped by Dunk Eldridge. We were both taking Morton Smith's course in Gnosticism and Dunk wanted to know what I thought of Clement of Alexandria's letter against the Carpocratians that Smith had dis- covered. There were rumors that it was a forgery, though the accusations that Smith himself was the forger only came later.

We batted it around. Dunk was the son of a small-town minister and looked like one, but he was smart. It took a while for us to notice that we were standing by ourselves. From the next room, where the couch had been pushed back against the wall, came handclaps. Someone shouted, "Go, baby!" People were watching from the doorway. We joined them.

You were dancing by yourself.

The other dancers had dropped out. You gave no sign of hearing anyone. It was twist music, but you weren't twisting. You weren't dancing to it at all. It was dancing in you. It ran through you like wind in a tree. It tossed you this way and that, wild but rooted. When you stopped, you stopped all at once, as if waking from a trance. Someone made room for you on the couch and you fell onto it. You were brought a glass of wine and took a sip.

I've seen real trance dancers – in the Caribbean, once in a Pentecostal church in Burma. They weren't like you at all. The only dancer who ever reminded me of you was in a little café in Upper Egypt. A large beaker of Turkish coffee was warming in hot coals; a moon had risen above the Nile, dappling the tourist bus parked beneath a tree. A man was playing a primitive stringed instrument. You couldn't call what he played a tune. It was more a sequence of rough twangs that might have come from a time before music was invented.

A boy rose to dance. He was tall with black ringlets and a tattered gray peasant's cloak. The soles of his feet were the color of earth. He held a staff that appeared to change shape as he danced. It was as though each time it led him into an impossible position, following it beyond where gravity could sustain him, it stretched or curved just enough for him to go on. He chose his steps with the concentration of a blind man, as if before him were hidden obstacles meant only for him. Afterwards he passed among the tables, slipping our coins into the pocket of his cloak while staring out over our heads, the heads of those who had not understood.

The record kept playing. A few dancers moved back onto the floor. Sam Bolowitz went over to you. "Come on, babe," he said. "Let's twist."

You smiled at him sweetly, "If you don't mind," you said, "I think I'll just sit here for a while."

"You can sit later," Bolowitz said. He grabbed your free hand and tried pulling you to your feet.

"Honestly," you said.

Bolowitz kept pulling.

"Look," you said, "if you're going to be such a creep, why don't you just crawl away?"

He let go of your hand. "Fucking bitch!" he said. "You can suck my cock, you fucking bitch! I'll bet you're good at it."

From the corner of my eye, I saw Ricky come over. He stepped between the two of you. "Why don't you leave her alone, pal," he said. "Go cool off."

"Move or I'll punch your fucking face in," Bolowitz said.

"You wouldn't want to do that," Ricky said. He kept his hands at his sides.

Bolowitz swung. Ricky's nose took the punch and he fell backwards. More astounding than the sight of him flying into your lap was your glass of wine sailing through the air in a perfect arc a split second before he landed. Athletes have reflexes like that. But they train for what they do and you had never before flipped a glass over your shoulder to keep a hurtling body from crushing it against you. It shattered against the wall, the stains of wine darker than the blood that spurted from Ricky's nose.

Bolowitz stood inspecting his hand for damage. He seemed unsure it was his; perhaps he hoped we would be, too. Danny Tutton took him by the arm and led him away. Ricky cupped his nose in both hands. The blood dripped through his fingers onto his shirt. He was made to lie on the couch with his head propped on pillows. Linda brought a towel from the bathroom and spread it over him. She handed you a washcloth to staunch the blood.

"Rick, are you all right?" you asked.

He grunted. His thin, fine nose, which was already beginning to swell, was smashed like a dropped piece of porcelain.

"You'd better get him to an emergency room," I said.

You made no move to get up. You looked depleted.

"Can you walk?" I asked Ricky. It was only a few blocks to St. Luke's.

He nodded. Fresh blood bubbled into the washcloth.

"Let's go," I said. "Come on, Mellie."

We took the elevator to the street and walked to Amsterdam Avenue and up it to St. Luke's. Ricky kept the washcloth pressed to his nose like a big blue handkerchief. My mood had improved. That prick Bolowitz had done wonders for it.

"Does it hurt?" you asked.

"Yes," Ricky said. "He shouldn't have hit me."

It sounded like "He shuddidabibbee."

"You should have bit him first," you said.

The emergency room was calm. A family stood whispering by one of the beds, most of which were empty. "You're in luck," a nurse said. "Some nights you need a reservation."

She gave Ricky a bed and covered him with a blanket. His nose had stopped bleeding. One side of his face was bright red, the other pale white; he looked like one of those soccer fans who paint themselves their team's colors. A young doctor with a clipboard came to examine him. "It looks like a multiple," he said. "We'll have to take an X-ray." Ricky said nothing. The doctor uncapped his pen. "Well, which was it?" he asked us. "Did he run into a wall or fall down the stairs?"

"Both," you said. "Simultaneously."

The doctor wrote something on the clipboard and left. We sat by the bed. It was almost midnight. You were thirsty. I went to the Coke machine at the end of the corridor. When I returned, Ricky had been taken to radiology.

We shared a Coke from a paper cup.

"Poor Ricky," you said. "He was very proud of his nose."

"It was quite Grecian," I said.

35

"What do you think it will look like now?"

"Probably Jewish."

You giggled. "This is like that night in Philadelphia."

"Not really." I rattled the ice at the bottom of the cup. "I didn't know the two of you were in New York."

"Since last summer," you said. "Ricky was in India. I'm in grad school at Columbia."

"So am I."

"I know," you said. "I saw you in the stacks at Butler."

"You did?"

"Yes. Oh, Hoo, I'm sorry!"

"You should be," I said. "You might at least have said hello."

"Not for that."

"For what?"

You bit your bottom lip.

"That summer?"

"Yes."

"You knew I knew?"

"When I called that Thanksgiving. I thought Ricky must have told you."

"He couldn't have," I said. "I never saw him again after that. I found a note of yours on the kitchen floor. There were dirty dishes in the sink too, but I didn't check them for fingerprints."

"We had a fight and left in a hurry. You were coming back that day. Ricky was about to sail on some freighter. I asked him not to. I begged him to come with me to Chicago. He wouldn't."

"Of course not. He had his heart set on being a bhikshu."

"We ended up screaming at each other. He sailed without saying goodbye. A couple of months ago I ran into him in the West End Bar & Grill. We started seeing each other. He's changed, Hoo. He had a very spiritual experience in India."

36

"I hate that word."

"There's nothing wrong with it."

"It's blah–blah."

"That's silly."

"You betrayed me."

"We betrayed ourselves."

"Why?"

"Why did we do anything then? Because we were even more frightened of everything else. Each of us was so alone."

"We still are."

"Yes. But don't you sometimes think we're learning to break through?"

"I'm a slow learner, Mellie. What are you in?"

"English lit. The Romantics."

"You danced beautifully."

"I danced ridiculously. I shouldn't have had that scotch. I must have looked like a fool."

"You didn't."

"I did. Hoo?"

"What?"

"I still have my ring."

You showed it to me.

"It's cracked," I said.

A thin line split the jade.

"It's just a scratch," you said. "Nicked by a mixer. Never whip cream without your work gloves. Aren't you glad, though?"

★

Ricky's nose was operated on. Although it was no longer Grecian, it didn't look Jewish either. It looked as if the surgeon had forgotten to sand it when he was done.

Who doesn't go to India these days? You visit Rishikesh or Dharmsala, you spend time in an ashram, you come home to work on your chakras. I know people who have done it a dozen times.

Back then, though, Ricky was the first. He must have told you more than he told me. This was that he jumped ship in Bombay. He found a cheap hotel near Chowpatty Beach, wandered the city for several days, and took the boat trip to Elephanta Island. In front of the statue of the triple-headed Shiva, he struck up a conversation with a man to whom he mentioned his interest in Vedanta. The man wrote the name and address of a teacher on a slip of paper and Ricky glanced at it and stuck it in his pocket.

He bought a guide book to India and traveled by train to Aurangabad and from there to Varanasi. He mingled with the crowds along the Ganges and saw the cremations by the ghats. Then he walked to the end of the city and kept on walking into the countryside of Uttar Pradesh. He walked by day and slept in villages at night. If he couldn't find someone who knew some English, a schoolteacher or government clerk, he got by on the smattering of Hindi he had begun to pick up. The land was flat, endless. It was the dry Indian winter. The dirt roads were packed hard by feet, hooves, the wheels of oxcarts. He bought sandals and gave away his shoes. He stopped shaving and let his hair grow long. He traded his knapsack for a blanket in which he kept his few possessions, wrapping himself in it at night. One night his money was stolen while he slept. After that he had to beg for food and lodgings. Faster than he had intended, he had become the bhikshu of his imaginings.

It surprised him how many people took him in and fed him without questions. The less they had, the more they were ready to share it. He headed north, using the sun as a compass. He discarded his guidebook; none of the places he was passing through were mentioned there anyway. His first glimpse of the Himalayas was mistaken by him for morning clouds on the horizon. But the day was hot and cloudless and the purple mass on the horizon remained. Each day it grew clearer, whiter-crested. He was walking in hills now. The nights were cold, the villages further apart. Often he slept beneath a tree. He could have used another blanket.

One day he came to a fork in the road. The sun was on his left. He was about to turn right when he noticed a sign pointing the other way. It reminded him of something. Reaching into his pocket, he found the crumpled note from Elephanta Island. On it was the name of the village on the sign.

He took the left-hand turn. The road climbed a hill and passed through a pine forest. Although he didn't break stride when he heard the wheels of an oxcart behind him, the driver stopped and offered him a ride. There were milk cans in the back of the cart and he squeezed in among them. After a while, the cart left the road and jolted up a pitted track. It stopped by a brick bungalow. The driver carried a can of milk to the front door. A man in a dhoti stepped out and paid him for it. "*Dhanyavaad, Swamiji*," the driver said, bowing. The man said to Ricky in a British-accented English:

"Well, here you are at last! You look a sight."

This was how he met his guru, Swami Vijñanananda. He had no way to account for it. Perhaps a letter had arrived from the man on Elephanta Island. But this still did not explain how, in a country with a hundred thousand villages, his feet had led him to the one whose forgotten name was in his pocket. A shad or salmon, he thought, must feel the same way when after years of blindly swimming the oceans it finds itself, drawn by an unsuspected force, at the mouth of the river that has been its destination all along.

Swami Vijñanananda was that force. The son of a wealthy Brahmin family from Orissa and a mathematical prodigy as a child, he had gone off to Oxford at the age of sixteen. Two years later, back in India on vacation, he attended a lecture by Swami Akhandananda, a former disciple of the renowned Sri Ramakrishna. He never returned to England. He gave up mathematics, moved to West Bengal where Akhandananda was teaching, and sat at his feet for many years. Then, taking his sunnyasa vows, he lived the life of a wandering mendicant until he came to the foothills of the Himalayas. There he settled down and began to teach.

Ricky entered the brick bungalow. Further up the hillside, the swami told him, were some thatch huts, to one of which he would be shown. This would be his lodging. There was a communal washroom and toilet. Meals were taken together. Apart from that, his time was his own. When he felt ready to begin his studies, he should return to the bungalow.

Ricky knocked on the door of the bungalow the next day. This time, Swami Vijñanananda asked him about himself. The words poured from him; he had barely spoken to anyone in weeks. He told the swami about growing up in New York, about his parents, about his childhood, about his high school, about his first encounter with books, about reading the Bhagavad Gita, about the skidding car in Colorado. Swami Vijñanananda listened and said:

"Your wish to learn is sincere, but your mind is too cluttered. Where will you put what I teach you? Go to your hut, rid yourself of all the thoughts you don't need, and come back."

Ricky went to his hut. The next days were tedious. He had never realized how busy his mind was, how it went from thought to thought like a fly buzzing around a room. Although only a minute had passed each time he glanced at his watch, his mind had already been in a dozen places. Thoughts were not guidebooks or shoes. The harder he tried to get rid of them, the more stubbornly they clung to him. Afraid to be told he would have to leave the ashram, he returned to the bungalow to report his failure.

"Now," said Swami Vijñanananda, "you're ready to begin."

And so Ricky became Swamiji's pupil. He was given a Hindi name – Jagvahiri, the far-traveling one. He exchanged his western clothes for a dhoti. He stored his watch with his few belongings in the straw chest by his mat and lost all sense of time. The dry season was followed by the monsoons, dripping from the thatch roof of his hut; the rains passed and it was winter again. He learned to meditate and do yoga, to control his breathing and his thoughts, to make his mind like the tip of a flame. That was a favorite image of his guru. Think of the body as a flame and the mind as its tip. When the flame burns steadily, with no draft from the windows or doors, its tip is calm and still. It doesn't flicker or flare. Difficult to master, this was the one-pointedness of samprajñata samadhi.

But there was a stage beyond that. A flame was most visible in darkness. Where there was light and darkness, there was duality. Having become a still flame, one had to learn to blow it out. This was the void of asamprajñata, in which there was no this and no that, no subject and no object, no self and no non-self.

His private sessions with his guru, Ricky supposed, owed something to the tutorials Swamiji had attended at Oxford. Not all of them concerned his spiritual progress. The other pupils on the hillside spoke only Hindi. Swami Vijñanananda missed speaking English and would invite Ricky to the brick bungalow, where they sat sipping mango juice or lemonade on the veranda in summer and hot tea by the fireplace in winter. He had a large library of English books from which he encouraged Ricky to borrow, and they would talk about the Christianity of Tolstoy, the mysticism of Meister Eckhart, or the *élan vital* of Henri Bergson, which bore a resemblance to the jiva of Hinduism.

Swami Vijñanananda lent Ricky *Alice In Wonderland*. Alice's falling down the rabbit hole, he said, could be a description of the beginning Vedanta student's disorientation as he grew aware of the illusions of consciousness. Ricky remarked that his dog Pinky would have made a natural Vedantist, since descending rabbit holes was a terrier's métier. Swami Vijñanananda laughed and wondered whether, had Charles Dodgson applied his mathematical knowledge to his metaphysical insights, he might have hit on the theory of relativity before Einstein.

They had a special relationship. Still, Ricky was unprepared when Swami Vijñanananda informed him one day that he wished to make him his successor. He had had many pupils, Swamiji said. Some had stayed with him for longer and some for shorter periods; some had progressed more than others. None, however, had the depth or breadth to absorb all his teachings. He was getting on in years. It was time to think of passing on his mantle. Ricky was the disciple he deemed most capable of donning it.

Ricky was stunned. He had barely been in the ashram three years. He was its youngest pupil. He had no real knowledge of Hindu culture. He could not read Sanskrit or study the scriptures in it. How could he be his guru's heir?

Swami Vijñanananda listened patiently. Ricky's doubts, he said, were understandable. Yet they needn't stand in his way if he had the determination to overcome them. It would take many more years of study and meditation. This was why he shouldn't wait any longer to take his sunnyasa vows. If he didn't feel equal to the task, now was the time to decide.

Ricky returned to his hut, feeling elated. For an hour his ego gorged on Swamiji's words like a dieter celebrating good news with a meal he knows will cost him extra effort to work off. When he finally sat down to meditate, it took him longer than usual to settle into his ordinary concentration. Several times his breathing lost its rhythm. Childish fantasies – of life in the brick bungalow, of the oxcart driver bowing to him as he delivered a can of milk, of welcoming a new pupil mysteriously arrived from afar – ran through his mind. He let them come and go, abject actors on a paltry stage. Gradually, his breathing grew regular. He slowly formed himself into a flame. Its warmth spread through his thighs, rose up the ridge of his spine, burned brightly in the cavity of his skull. He let it shine there, pure and radiant. Then, on the next exhalation, he bent to blow it out. Too late, he realized he had been hasty. The breath failed to leave his lungs smoothly. The flame wobbled, danced prankishly. It teetered and fell like a candle on a table knocked over by a careless hand. The tablecloth caught fire. Before he could stamp out the flames, they had spread to the rest of the hut. A curtain began to burn; then the straw chest and the shelf on the wall. He ran to save a book on the shelf. The flames cut him off. He turned and raced for the door, reaching it as the thatch roof combusted.

Only when he flung the door open and breathed the gray morning air, in which the first clouds of the coming monsoons

hid the snow-capped mountains to the north, did he realize he
had had a waking nightmare. A myna bird darted from a pine
tree. The pines gave off a dark, dusty smell. He forced himself to
turn around and look back, half-expecting to see his hut reduced
to cinders. It was still there. The tablecloth lay on the table. The
faded curtain hung on the window. On the shelf on the wall was
the illustrated volume of *Vanity Fair* lent him by Swami
Vijñanananda.

He returned to his mat and tried to resume meditating. His
agitation was too great. He went to the brick bungalow and told
Swamiji what had happened.

"What made you want to rescue the book?" Swami
Vijñanananda asked.

Ricky shut his eyes and tried picturing the scene: the burning
hut, the heavy, illustrated volume. But it wasn't *Vanity Fair.* It was
a photograph album. It had sat in a cabinet in his parents' living
room, between his bronzed baby shoes and his mother's
collection of little glass animals that he had loved to play with as
a child. In it were pictures from his childhood, from before it: of
his mother in a summer dress standing by a baby carriage, his
father arm-wrestling in the sand at the seashore, young men and
women he couldn't identify.

"A Western psychologist," Swami Vijñanananda said, "would
say you were hallucinating – experiencing an eruption of your
unconscious or dreaming mind that ordinary consciousness was
unable to contain. He would consider this a malfunction of consciousness, perhaps even a sign of mental disturbance. In most
cases, he might be right. But we know that ordinary
consciousness is a form of dreaming, too. Our goal is to awake
from it. Svapna, jakrata, turiya: the dreaming of the unconscious
mind, the dreaming of the conscious mind, the state of

wakefulness. These are three rungs of a ladder. If the rung you are standing on suddenly gives way, you either rise to the next one or fall to the one beneath it. This time you fell. In itself, this is no reason for concern."

Swami Vijñanananda was concerned for another reason. Although Western psychology understood consciousness differently, its analysis of dream symbols was sound. The album stood for Ricky's sense of identity, composed of his life and memories. The thought of stepping into his guru's shoes had made him frightened of losing it. "I can't promise you that you won't," Swami Vijñanananda said. "No one can take away from you who you are. But if you remain with me, the person you once were will recede as surely as land recedes from a ship that has put to sea. Go back to New York, Ricky. See if this person still matters. Then decide if you wish to continue the voyage."

And so Ricky returned to New York. It took him less time than it had taken to travel the other way. Once he received the Western Union money order sent him by Ralph Silverman, he took a jitney cab to Shahjahanpur, a train to New Delhi, and a TWA flight to Idlewild that touched down briefly in Istanbul.

*

Ricky told me all this one morning when I came to lend you my copy of *Under The Volcano*. It was just beginning to be talked about then.

You and I had met a few times since Moysh's party. Once you called me; once we ran into each other on campus. I told you about Harvard, about Robin. You told me about Chicago. You had had a serious relationship with someone, too. He brought you to his North Shore home to meet his parents. On a mantel stood a photograph, so you thought, of him as a teenager that

45

turned out to be of his father, a bald, jovial man with a belly. You broke up with him soon afterwards.

We talked again about that summer. "I was in love with you both," you said. "You were shy and Ricky wasn't." You had never slept with anyone before. "Ricky was about to ship out," you said. "We wanted to spend a few days together. We were afraid a hotel would turn us away. Neither of us even had a driver's license. There was no way we could have told you that."

You were living in an apartment building on the corner of 106th and Broadway. It was my first time there. The elevator was slow. It took so long to open when it reached your floor that I almost pressed the alarm.

You had told me that you would be home and that Ricky had a yoga class to teach at the Buddhist Center on Riverside Drive, but it was he who came to the door when I rang. His class had been canceled and you had had to go somewhere. Although I wanted to hand him the book and get back into the elevator, he insisted I come in. Afterwards, I wondered if you hadn't planned it that way.

I had never been anywhere you lived. At the time, I couldn't have said what was so special about it. Today, I would call it the contentment of things. The hand-woven Navaho rug, the round table with its bowl of apples and its white rose in a thin-necked vase, the three crows in a painting on the wall done by a college friend, the rubber plant glossy in its corner, the wicker bookcase with its poets that you loved, Rilke and Neruda and Yeats and Dylan Thomas: everything was happy to be where you had put it. There wasn't a single complaint.

A stick of incense was burning on the top shelf of the bookcase. Ricky excused himself for sitting on the rug. He was more comfortable that way, he said. It was awkward facing him

46

from a chair and I dropped to the floor, too, and leaned against a pillow. He took that to mean I was in no hurry. The incense had burned down before he finished telling me about India. I asked:

"So? Does that person still matter?"

He measured me. I wondered whether, when meditating, he now focused on the bump on his nose.

"He's elusive, that person. Mellie tells me he still matters to you, though."

"Shouldn't he?"

"Not if he's no longer around to answer the question."

"You could try answering it for him."

"I could. But you and I would both be proxies. Neither of us is who he was then."

"Speak for yourself," I said. "I'm still me."

"That's an illusion of consciousness, pal."

"Everything is an illusion of consciousness. You didn't have to go to India to find that out. We knew it when we were children. The world is a trick played on us by subatomic particles. That didn't keep your nose from hurting when Sam Bolowitz broke it."

"Swami Vijñanananda has a story about that. A man hears a guru say that everything is maya. One day he's walking down a road and sees an elephant coming toward him. Since the elephant is maya, he thinks, there's no need to get out of its way. The elephant knocks him down and nearly kills him. He goes back to the guru to complain that elephants aren't maya after all. 'Oh, but they are!' the guru says. 'And the next time you see a maya-elephant coming down a maya-road, get your maya-ass out of its maya-way.'"

"Samuel Johnson made the same point by kicking a stone at Bishop Berkeley," I said. "He should have kicked Berkeley. If we have to treat our illusions as real, it's an illusion to think they're illusions."

"On some level they are."

"Which level were you on in my parents' bed?"

He stuck a finger in his nose and dabbed it on your Navaho rug. "Oh, fuck it, man," he said. "You want an apology?" He joined his palms and bowed with mock gravity. "My maya-self asks your maya-self's forgiveness."

He grinned his old grin, the one I first saw on that day in the lunchroom when I told him he was full of shit.

★

It was during the months I was going out with Cora – there weren't many of them – that we fought the world war. You made dinner. Rob and Cindy Moses brought a new board game. Cora and I brought the wine. "She's stunning," you whispered to me.

She was, those big green eyes of hers especially. They had brown and gold flecks like sunlight on fallen leaves. A few years ago I met her in New York at a book party for an author we both knew. The afterglow of her beauty hadn't entirely faded. We stood in a corner and talked. She had never married. She had always known, she said, that she wasn't made for one man. The list of her lovers was impressive. It included a legendary jazz pianist, a Pulitzer prize-winning poet, and an internationally known French postmodernist philosopher. I said I was flattered to have been the Ganymede in such a Pantheon, and she laughed and ran warm fingers through my hair. Had she lived in other times, she would have been a famous courtesan.

Rob explained the rules of the game. The board had a map of pre-World War I Europe. We would each be a country with an

48

army and a navy that could be moved one square at a time. Between moves, countries could negotiate, forge alliances, and intrigue against each other. No country had to keep its promises. We could dissemble, deceive, and double-cross, just as in real life. The goal was to conquer all of Europe.

We drew lots. Cora was Turkey. Ricky was England. You were France and I was Italy. We moved our armies to their frontiers and broke for talks. You came over to me and said, "Hoo, I don't think I like this game."

"*Madame l'ambassadrice française*," I said to you, "let us put aside the childish names of our youth. I must ask you to address me as Admiral Hugo Cipellino-Tortini, the Italian minister of war."

You looked at me. Before my eyes you became the French ambassador to Rome. "*Mais vous avez tout á fait raison, monsieur l'amiral*," you said. "We are no longer children throwing snowballs on the slopes of St. Moritz."

"Those days were charming," I said. "But now we must steer a wise course through the tempests of war. *Al più potente cede il più prudente*, we Italians say, but it is the prudent who survive in the end."

"*Eh bien*," you said, "why not join power and prudence together? I propose an eternal treaty of friendship between France and Italy."

Russia and Turkey were huddled at one end of the room, Germany, Austria, and England at the other. "*Ma chére ambassadrice*," I said, "what is eternity? It is less time than it takes a Sunday dinner to end in the eyes of a child. And a check for ten francs that must be honored by a bank is worth more than a treaty between nations."

"Does Italy doubt the honor of France?" you asked.

"Italy has cause to," I said. "Did not Louis-Philippe stab us in

49

the back with Metternich? You drank champagne with him in Paris while his troops crushed us in Modena."

"Your knowledge of history is admirable," you said. "But history must sometimes be forgotten."

"Shall we burn the books in which it is written?" I asked. "You will excuse me, *madame*. I believe your Turkish colleague would like a word with me."

Cora proposed a non-aggression pact. I believed her and soon found myself in a Turkish–Austrian vise. She and Moysh, plotting behind my back, invaded Italy from two directions. I retreated to Rome while appealing to Russia for a diversionary attack on the Bosporus. The Tsar was too occupied with Germany to comply. With French intervention my only hope, I rushed to Paris.

You were scornful. "Had you accepted my offer last autumn, *monsieur l'amiral*," you said, "you would not have had to come begging now."

"*Dio santo!*" I said. "Are we going to argue about last autumn when the Hapsburgs and Saracens are at the gates of Rome?"

"Paris," you said, "is more concerned with the rumors of a Russian–German entente" – and off you went to talk to the Hapsburgs and Saracens. I chatted idly with England while watching the three of you confer.

My situation seemed hopeless. Yet when autumn came again, you risked shifting a division from the German front to threaten the Austrian flank. The Austrians withdrew beyond the Alps to meet the threat and Rome was saved. We spoke again on your next visit.

"Italy is indebted," I said. "Please convey my country's gratitude to your government."

"I hope, *monsieur*," you said, "that French honor has been restored."

"If France's offer still stands," I said, "Italy will be pleased to accept it."

"When Italy is pleased, France is delighted," you said.

We went down to a swift defeat. The rumored entente took place and the Germans turned westward and struck at France with superior forces. Sending a doomed fleet through the Straits of Gibraltar to your aid, I lost control of the Aegean to the Turks. My navy was sunk off the Spanish coast by England, which joined the German attack when your ships tried coming to my rescue. "France stands by its friends," you declared. The Russians were now ready to move against Turkey if I abandoned you. I sent their ambassador packing.

We were the first two countries to surrender. While the war went on, we sat in the kitchen drinking tea. You told me you had decided to write your M.A. thesis on Keats. "He's a sweetheart," you said.

"He died young enough to remain one," I said. "Sometimes I think I will too."

"Don't die before me, Hoo," you said.

"If I do," I said, "we'll arrange to meet somewhere. Do you remember the argument about Keats I had with Ricky in that Chinese restaurant?"

"Of course I do," you said. "You dropped your food in your tea."

"I was right."

"You were?"

"Yes."

"I always knew it!" you said.

I broke up with Cora a few weeks later, during the Cuban missile crisis.

★

The two of us wouldn't have lasted long anyway, but the missile crisis cut it even shorter. Cora wanted me to go with her to a demonstration at the United Nations. I said I had reading to do. She was incredulous. "You're going to die in a nuclear war and you want to *read*?"

"At least I'll die doing what I like," I said.

"This isn't a joke."

"A demonstration won't save humanity."

"You don't give a shit for humanity."

She went to the demonstration, met an Australian journalist, and threw me over for him.

I knew how she felt. Once, in first grade, I had a fight with a boy from a higher class. He was a fat boy with freckles, and he told me that his father had brought home a hand grenade from the war and that he was going to bring it to school and blow me up. I was terrified. I told my mother that I wasn't going to school any more. She asked me why. I said a boy was going to kill me with a hand grenade. She put her arm around me and explained that I needn't worry, because soldiers didn't bring home live hand grenades and certainly didn't give them to their children. It was what any sensible parent would have said and I thought: *she doesn't understand. He'll kill me and she doesn't understand.*

I returned to first grade, but I never again made the mistake of thinking that grown-ups knew anything or that there was any point in telling them a thing.

We all learned not to make it. Do you remember those drills in which we had to crawl under our desks and cover our heads against an atom bomb? Who of us imagined for a moment that a world that had invented a bomb to kill us all and was pretending a desk top would protect us could be taken seriously?

The sixties started then. Not with *Howl* or *On The Road,* or with the Greensboro sit-ins, or with the Kennedy assassination. With that. It was the sleeping agent that the missile crisis awoke. There was all that talk about how young Kennedy was. But he was old enough to be our father and as ready to kill us over Cuba as Khrushchev was. Both played with our lives as though we were pieces in a board game.

We were the young. Adulthood was a stupidity we wanted nothing to do with. It just took years to discover that what each of us had thought was a private resolution belonged to us all.

It began in high school. Our little group was like the cell of a revolutionary party that has no inkling of the conspiracy it is part of. All that was needed to make the sixties possible was for the cells to begin to link up. You were right. We were breaking through.

The revolution of the proletariat of the young! The unbelievable thing was how many of us believed it.

That time at Rob and Cindy's, do you remember? They were living in the East Village, in a walk-up on Avenue B. It was a muggy summer night. Cats shot out of the garbage pails like rockets. The empty beer cans tossed through the open windows of the tenements popped on the sidewalks like cap pistols. In Chicago, the Yippies were rioting at the Democratic convention. We were listening to Country Joe and the Fish while drinking beer and smoking pot and talking about buying land in the country. Moysh and Linda were there. So was Eve Trager with her boyfriend and some friend of Rob's who taught history at Horace Mann or Dalton. A siren was wailing. There were sirens all the time in New York. The city was full of ambulances, fire engines, police cars, muggers, purse-snatchers, pushers, psychopaths, drunks, demonstrators, beggars, Hare Kirshnas, three-card monte players, people talking to themselves. The parks were more dangerous than Vietnam.

The history teacher said, "It's coming. The military–industrial complex is finished."

"Where the hell do you think we are," Moysh asked, "in Petrograd in 1917?"

"No, man," said the teacher. "This is Bloody Sunday, 1905. I give the system ten more years."

"In ten years," Moysh said, "Abbie Hoffman and Jerry Rubin will be running the Yippy Frozen Yoghurt Company with franchises in all fifty states."

"Forget about Abbie and Jerry," the teacher said. "I'm talking about the next generation. You should listen to the kids I teach. Soon they'll be blowing up the power structure with real dynamite."

Beer cans. Sirens. Country Joe and the Fish. Five minutes later there was banging on the door. Rob opened it and three guys and a girl dashed in and slammed it behind them.

"We did it!" yelled one of them. He wore a motorcycle jacket and had a pony tail. "We trashed the fucking pig pen, man!"

He smelled of kerosene. They had smashed a window of the police station on East 5th Street with a brick, he said, and lobbed a Molotov cocktail after it. "You should have seen the fucking smoke! I bet we killed a pig."

I glanced at you. You were staring at him. He went to the bathroom to wash up and we rose to go. Rob and Cindy begged us to stay. They were freaked by the thought of being accessories to the murder of a policeman. So were we. In the street I asked:

"Was I imagining it?"

"No," you said. "It was Peter."

My friend Peter Spatz, who passed me clever notes in

Caroline Ames' writing class. He was too stoned to recognize us.

The next morning I scanned the *Times*. On a back page was a brief item about an incendiary device that had hit a wall of the 9th Precinct police station in Manhattan and done no damage.

We stayed on the margins of it all. Today, that seems like wisdom. Back then, it felt more like timidity. We stood on the bank and watched the current carry lives to improbable places. Peter Spatz became a Weatherman and did time for a bomb in the New York Stock Exchange that luckily failed to go off. Moysh never finished his dissertation; he dropped out of graduate school, found a job teaching remedial English, and turned into a Republican crank. Rob and Cindy split up: Rob cut his golden locks and went into his father's furniture business and Cindy – fresh-as-dew Cindy from Milford, Connecticut! – had a child with a black actor who abandoned her, moved to a commune in Vermont, and vanished for years until Danny Tutton came across her living on welfare in Oakland. Dunk Eldridge had his brains fried by acid. Eve Trager's boyfriend fled to Canada to evade the draft and left her with a baby monkey that died of pneumonia.

And then there was Ricky.

You were worried about him. At first I thought it was only because of Vietnam. Whoever didn't have a student deferment was in trouble. Rob got a 3-A by pretending to be the father of Cindy's child. Moysh got one, too; he deposited half his monthly paycheck in the bank account of his retired parents, had it returned to him in cash, and claimed them as dependents. Danny Tutton found a psychiatrist to write a note stating he was unfit for military service.

Ricky didn't want to tell any lies. "He's decided to file as a conscientious objector," you told me.

"I hope he knows what he's doing," I said. "I'm not sure he meets the requirements."

"I know," you said. "But it's what Swami Vijñanananda told him to do."

"He heard from him?"

"By mental message."

Whatever message Ricky had gotten, it was risky. Draft boards didn't like c.o. applicants. Most were turned down.

Ricky went to his draft board. As he later described it to me, he was interviewed by a committee of three.

"They were sitting around a big table. Each had a notepad with a sharpened pencil in front of him. Before my father went to work for the city, he had a job with an accounting firm called McGarrity, Tompkins & Grant, and that's how I thought of them. McGarrity was in the dark suit, Tompkins was in the gray suit, and Grant was in the blue blazer. McGarrity was the committee head. He wanted to know why I objected to military service. I said it was because of my religious beliefs. He asked what beliefs those were. I said they were the beliefs of Hinduism and Tompkins says, 'Hinduism! Isn't that idol worship?'

"Go explain Vedanta to three tight-assed dudes who think a Quaker meeting is subversive. I tried, and they wrote on their pads, and after a while Tompkins interrupts me and says, 'Mr. Silverman, this is all a bit abstruse. Tell me frankly: do you believe in God?'

"I say to him, 'It depends on what you mean by that.' He says, 'I mean a supreme being.' I say, 'How about an ultimate reality?' and he says, 'Do you pray to it?'

"I say, 'Oh, no. That would be like praying to myself.'

"Grant puts his elbows on the table and says, 'Mr. Silverman, are you telling us that *you* are the ultimate reality?'

"I say, 'I'm telling you that you are.'

"They wrote some more. Then McGarrity wants to know why the ultimate reality is opposed to war. I say, 'Because we're all part of it. Killing you is killing me.'"

"You're lucky they never read the Bhagavad Gita," I said. "That's not what Krishna tells Arjuna."

"No, Arjuna, it isn't. But Krishna tells him to kill because he's a warrior. That's his caste. It's his karma, not mine. Anyway, I got through that part of it. It turned out there was more, though, because now I'm told that my beliefs aren't enough. They have to come from a religious tradition I've been trained in.

"I told them I trained in India for over three years with a guru. They looked at me as if that were the name of a Himalayan bird. I explained what a guru was and Tompkins asks, 'What proof of such studies can you give us?'

"Now they want a parchment diploma! I'm about to tell them that Swami Vijñanananda didn't hand them out when I hear him say, 'Jagvahiri!' I say, 'Yes, Swamiji?' and he says, 'Do vrishchikasana!' That's the scorpion position. It's an arm stand with your back arched and your knees bent, so that the tips of your toes touch the top of your head. There are harder positions than that, but it's the hardest I ever learned to do properly. I say, 'Where?' It's a small room. He says, 'On the table.' I say, 'On the *table*?' He says, 'There's nowhere else,' so I take off my shoes and climb onto the table. McGarrity says, 'Mr. Silverman, just what do you think you're doing?' and I say, 'I'm giving you the proof you asked for' and do the best scorpion I can, which isn't perfect because I have all my clothes on. We're eyeball-to-eyeball with my legs in the air and I say, 'This, gentlemen, takes years of training.'"

57

"What happened then?"

"Nothing. McGarrity told me to get off the table in a voice you'd use with someone balancing on a tenth-floor windowsill. I did and they said I could go and would hear from them. They must have thought that in another minute I'd start levitating."

Ricky was asked to appear before a second committee. Then his exemption came in the mail. It wasn't the 1-O he had asked for. It was a 4-F like that given Danny Tutton.

3

I once said to you that, for as long as I loved him, Ricky was the only male friend I ever loved, and you said:

"You never stopped loving him. You just told yourself that you did."

"What I told myself," I said, "was that I had fallen behind. It started even before that summer, with that trip of his out west. We had always been neck-and-neck and he came back from it way ahead of me. Suddenly, I was looking up to him. I couldn't stand that."

"He looked up to you too," you said.

"That's hard to believe."

"He did. He thought you were the only person he knew who was smarter than he was."

"He said that?"

"We were talking about you. It was after that friend of Moysh's broke his nose."

"Sam Bolowitz."

"I sometimes think that's what unhinged him."

"A broken nose?"

"A balance. He had those two sides. There was a thin line between them — and it was smashed. He stood there and let himself be hit.... Look, maybe that had nothing to do with it. He could have been headed for a crash anyway."

"I was the last to see it," I said. "His draft board realized it before I did. Doing handstands on a table just seemed like Ricky to me. I didn't suspect anything until I went with him to that Tibetan temple in Brooklyn."

It was run by a monk named Tenzing Rinpoche with whom Ricky had been studying. Someone had donated a new scroll painting and Ricky was invited to a ceremony in its honor. I joined him out of curiosity. We took the train all the way to East Flatbush. Ricky brought a bouquet of flowers and sat holding it carefully in his lap. We must have looked like a suitor and his best man.

The temple was in a loft above a store that sold Tibetan hand-icrafts and religious artifacts. A dark flight of stairs led up to it. The painting hung behind an altar. It was of two brightly colored figures, each with an arm around the other's waist and the other arm brandishing a spear; underfoot, they trampled inky blue midgets. Ricky explained that they were Shiva and Shakti and that the midgets were the demons of the passions. Tinzeng Rinpoche belonged to the Vajrayana school, which made wide use of such symbols.

Ricky added his flowers to the pile on the altar. The loft smelled of the incense he had burned that day in your apartment. Tenzeng Rinpoche wore a red robe. A friendly man who dropped his final consonants, he was amused when Ricky tried getting me to bow to him. "So gla yu ku joi us," he said, shaking the hand I held out.

The ceremony was short. We held candles. There was slow Tibetan chanting. Someone rang a little bell and someone played a small two-headed drum shaped like an hour-glass, swiveling it to make its round wooden clappers beat against the drumheads like paddleballs. Afterwards there were pastries and Tibetan tea, which tasted like hot greasy pickle brine.

The train back to Manhattan was empty. Ricky looked preoc-cupied. I translated an ad for a preparation against hemorrhoids into Latin, then picked up a *Daily News* left on the seat beside me. I read a story about a two-headed calf born in Scotland and another about a man who had swallowed a gold tiepin in a hamburger, and I offered the paper to Ricky.

He waved it away. I translated the ad into Greek. A few stations later, he said:

"Whew. That was some argument."

"What was?"

"Swami Vijñanananda and Tenzing Rinpoche's."

"When?"

"Now."

"Where?" I didn't know what he was talking about.

"Here." He tapped his head.

"You imagined they were arguing?"

"No, Arjuna. They were arguing."

The argument was about him. "Swami Vijñanananda started it. He said Vajrayana wasn't for me. He said it claimed to be a shortcut but led to dangerous places. Tenzing Rinpoche said, 'It's you who takes shortcuts. You wanted Ricky to go straight to emptiness when a mind fed by impure streams fills as quickly as it empties.' Swami Vijñanananda answered, 'My way is pure,' and Tengzing Rinpoche said, 'You're like a yogi trying to cleanse the body just by fasting. Unless he practices the kriyas and purges his system, no cleansing will take place.'"

"You *heard* that?" I asked.

"It's not the first time," Ricky said. "They argue a lot. Swami Vijñanananda talks in his chai-chai Oxford English and Tinzeng Rinpoche with his Tibetan accent. Sometimes they shout. It gives me a headache."

At 42nd Street, we shuttled to the IRT. I got off at 96th and thought, I have to talk to Mellie.

★

You phoned before I did. We met at the Red Chimney on 103rd Street. "What's up?" I asked.

"Too much," you said.

I said, "That's better than too little."

"Not this time," you said. "I'm having trouble with my adviser, Ricky is acting strangely, and I. . ." You ran a finger around the rim of the sugar pourer. "I'm pregnant. I need an abortion."

"How pregnant?"

"In my second month."

"Does Ricky know?"

"Yes."

"What does he say?"

"He wants me to have the baby."

"Is he. . ."

". . .ready to marry me? He says so, but I don't think he means it. I couldn't marry him anyway. Not the way he is now."

"I wanted to talk to you about that," I said. I told you about our trip to Brooklyn.

"He's into all this Tantra stuff," you said. "The whole apartment is full of statues and mandalas. He spends hours in front of them."

"Doing what?"

"God knows. Meditating. Chanting. Playing weird Tibetan instruments. It's creepy."

"What does he want a baby for?"

"That's the creepiest part."

Two small quotation marks I had never seen before appeared in your forehead when you frowned.

"You saw that painting of Shiva and Shakti. He's the masculine principle of the universe and she's the feminine. It's a Yin–Yang sort of thing. In Tantra you identify with gods and demons. You project your inner self onto them so that detachment from it is easier. Tinzeng Rinpoche told Ricky to visualize himself as Shiva. That makes me Shakti. It makes the baby some kind of god, too."

"Congratulations," I said.

"I don't need your sarcasm. Ricky won't hear of aborting it. But I can't have it, Hoo. There's no way."

"Where would you go for an abortion?"

"I talked to Cindy. She gave me the name of a doctor in New Hampshire. He's expensive but reliable."

"I can lend you money."

"I have money. I'll need someone to drive me."

"I'll ask Dunk Eldridge for his VW," I said. "What will you tell Ricky?"

"I'll think of something. What will you tell Dunk?"

"Something," I said.

You told Ricky you were going to Philadelphia for your Aunt Trude's sixtieth birthday party and I told Dunk I had heard of twenty-five acres for sale in New Hampshire that I wanted to take a look at. He was so excited by my account of the woods and the brook and all the raspberry and blueberry bushes that he offered me his Beetle before I asked for it and even drove it over with a full tank of gas. He was so tall and it was so small that he could have steered with his knees.

The doctor lived in a town called Keene. I had gotten hold of a roadmap and marked a route. At first, the car gave me trouble. I had never driven a floor shift and I stalled it twice before we hit the West Side highway. On the Henry Hudson, I downshifted by mistake from fourth to first and thought the engine would explode. Exiting the Saw Mill River for the Taconic, I got stuck in neutral and we almost had an accident.

"Hoo," you said, "keep this up and I won't need an abortion."

It took a while to get the hang of it. Even then you put a hand out toward the dashboard each time I braked. "It's a reflex from childhood," you said. "For a couple of summers, my parents rented a house on Martha's Vineyard. It was a step up from the bungalow colony we spent our vacations in before that. The second year, my father decided we needed a car. He took driving lessons and got his license and bought a second-hand Buick from a dealer, a shiny black sedan with a running board. The first time we went for a ride, he took a turn too fast and flipped it over. No one was hurt, but I've been scared of accidents ever since."

"When were you in the Vineyard?" I asked.

"It must have been. . . ." You thought. "In nineteen-forty-nine and 'fifty."

"You're kidding," I said. "I was there in forty-nine, too. We had a house on the water between Oak Bluffs and Vineyard Haven. That was the summer I learned to ride a bike. I could have biked right past you without knowing it."

"You probably did," you said. "I was the chubby girl with the braces on the bridge near Vineyard Haven."

"The one over the bay."

"Yes. There was a beach there we sometimes walked to."

"I used to stand on that bridge looking at the sailboats," I said. "My great dream was to sail one. What happened to the car?"

"Nothing. My father sold it back to the dealer and never drove again. I was too embarrassed to tell anyone about it. I thought all Americans drove cars and he couldn't because he came from Europe."

You were born in Antwerp. Your father was in the diamond business. Half a year before the German invasion, a sixth sense prompted him to sell everything and you moved to Paris just in time. When the Germans followed, you fled to Vichy and applied for an American visa. You had a cousin in New York who promised to arrange it. But your mother was from Hamburg and had a German passport, and the U.S. *chargé d'affaires* in Marseilles didn't think being Jewish made her less of an enemy national.

"She met my father when a dance troupe she was in performed in Antwerp," you said. "It was her idea to call me Melisande."

"I always wondered where that came from," I said.

"It's from a poem of Heine's, *Geoffroy Rudèl und Melisande von Tripoli*. Melisande was a countess married to a Crusader lord. Geoffroy was a French troubadour so smitten by the descriptions of her beauty that he set out from France for a glimpse of her. He fell ill aboard ship and arrived in Tripoli on the verge of death. Melisande heard that a dying poet was murmuring her name and hurried to see him. She fell in love with him at first sight and he died in her arms."

"Melisande von Tripoli," I said. "What makes me think I know her from somewhere?"

"In Heine's poem," you said, "Geoffroy and Melisande are in a tapestry hanging on a castle wall. One night when everyone is asleep, they step out of it and walk in the moonlight. Melisande says,

> *Geoffroy! Wir liebten uns*
> *Einst im Traume, und jetzunder*
> *Lieben wir uns gar im Tode —*
> *Gott Amor tat dieses Wunder,*

and Geoffroy answers,

> *Melisande! Was ist Traum?*
> *Was ist Tod? Nur eitel Töne.*

In der Liebe nur ist Wahrheit,
Und dich lieb ich, ewig Schöne."

You knew some German from your mother. When the round-ups of Jews began in Vichy, your father purchased Dominican *laissez-passers* and you sailed to Lisbon and from there on a freighter to Ciudad Trujillo. A year later, the U.S. visa came through. You were four. Your only memory of those years was of a stick of sugar cane given you to suck on in the Dominican Republic. When you sucked your thumb at night to help you fall asleep, you imagined it was sugar cane.

You were small for your age. You tired easily and were given cod liver oil. It was months before you spoke any English. Your mother listened to the radio a lot, and your first complete sentence, uttered when you went to fetch a doll, was "I'll be right back after this message."

Have I gotten it right so far, Mellie?

"It's odd," I said, "that the three of us are only children – you, Ricky, and me."

"That's why we take ourselves so seriously," you said. "We didn't have older brothers or sisters to take us down a peg or younger ones to upstage us. We had the confidence that we were all our parents wanted."

"And the worry that we would never be enough for them."

"And their fear that something would happen to us. I was scared all the time as a child."

"What's your scariest memory?" I asked.

"I saw a boy killed. He chased a ball into the street and was hit by a car. I ran home and shut myself up in my closet and wouldn't come out. I thought it was the only place where death couldn't find me. What's yours?"

66

We traded scariest and most embarrassing and happiest memories. Then we exchanged first ambitions. Yours was to be a ballet dancer. Mine was to be a garbage collector. "I wanted to ride on the back of a truck and wear leather gloves," I said. "I loved to watch them roll and swing the big tin cans. It was the sound of waking up in the morning."

"Your parents must have been overjoyed," you said.

"My mother let me know that garbage men earned poorly and that I should consider another profession. She's a social worker. She always thinks she has to be the voice of reason. She's the kind of parent who takes you to the movies and whispers to you at the height of the suspense not to worry because it isn't real."

"And your father?"

"He's an orthopedic surgeon at Mount Sinai. I get along better with him. The only bad fight we ever had was when I was applying for college. A colleague of his had moved to Boston and become friendly with the president of Harvard, and he wanted to ask him to put in a good word for me. I was furious. I told him not to dare. Either I got into Harvard on my own merits or I didn't want to get in at all. He called me a moron and we didn't talk for a week. When the acceptance letter came, I ran to show it to him. He read it and said, 'I apologize. If I had known Harvard accepted morons, I would never have called you one.'"

"Did it ever occur to you," you asked, "that you got into Harvard because he talked to his friend anyway?"

"No," I said. "And I intend to forget that it ever occurred to you."

"This is fun," you said. "It's the conversation we never had in high school."

We stopped for lunch in a diner on Route 22. It was a cold, windy day in early April. The trees were still bare. We ate BLT's and talked about your thesis. You were writing on Keats' "Ode to Psyche". It had always been treated as a poor sister to the other odes. But you were taking Lionel Trilling's course on the English romantics, and when Trilling said that Keats, as opposed to the common perception of him, was a man of ideas, you saw them there.

"Everyone thinks of him as a kind of sugarplum," you said. "Even Yeats called him a boy with his face pressed to the window of a sweetshop. But he wasn't, Hoo. He was tough-minded. The poems are just so gorgeous that no one notices. You read lines like,

> O Goddess! hear these tuneless numbers, wrung
>> By sweet enforcement and remembrance dear,
> And pardon that thy secrets should be sung
>> Even unto thine own soft-conchèd ear,

and they sound like a lot of taffeta and lace. You don't realize they're written by a brilliant intellect."

You thought "Ode to Psyche" was about the modern intellectual. "When he says to Psyche,

> Yes, I will be thy priest, and build a fane
>> In some untrodden region of my mind,
> Where branchèd thoughts, new grown with pleasant pain,
>> Instead of pines shall murmur in the wind,

he's talking about our doing for ourselves what religion once did for everyone. About creating a soul."

"A *psykhē*."

"He called the world a vale of soul-making. That may just sound like a well-turned phrase, but it's an extraordinary thing to have said. Souls were always thought to come from somewhere, from God or some pre-existent place. You didn't make your own. Even Wordsworth says, 'The soul that rises with us has elsewhere had its setting and cometh from afar.' Keats was talking about something new."

You were having a hard time convincing your adviser of that. "I met with Frank Gifford last week. He spent an hour telling me it's just a semantic confusion on my part. He said all Keats was doing was using the word soul for what eighteenth-century philosophers were already calling the self. He told me to read Hume's chapter on 'Personal Identity' in his *Treatise on Human Nature.*"

"Did you?"

"Yes. Hume says the self is no more than the sum of its parts. At bottom, we're nothing but an ongoing sequence of sense impressions, feelings, and thoughts. If we had no memory of them, we'd have no sense of identity. It's memory that gives our experience an illusion of continuity that we ascribe to an independent experiencer, just as a spectator in the theater ascribes the play he's watching to an author. It's just that the play really has an author, while we're the authors of our selves. Gifford thinks Keats is rehashing that idea in 'Ode to Psyche'. He's saying poetically what Hume said discursively."

"You don't think so."

"I think Hume is taking an early stab at a theory of ego formation. What he says about the self is pretty much what Ricky would say. Modern psychology and Eastern religion have a lot in common. Keats isn't talking about an ego. He's talking about an immortal soul."

69

"Made by mortals."

"Yes."

"How?"

"He doesn't say. It appears as a passing thought. His brother and sister-in-law had emigrated to America and he was writing them a letter in installments, adding lines or pages when he could. A lot of it is just news and London gossip. But at one point he mentions a book of Voltaire's that he's been reading, and suddenly – it just seems to pop into his head – he says we're all endowed with a natural capacity for thought and feeling and he asks, 'Do you not see how necessary a world of pains and troubles is to school an intelligence and make it a soul?' I showed that to Ricky. He said the only soul we have is the karmic one we're born with. I told him I didn't want a used soul. I hate second-hand clothes, so why should I want a second-hand soul? He said, 'Then go to the God of Christianity. He'll issue you a brand-new soul when you're born and you'll hand it back when you die for him to decide how dirty you've gotten it and if it's presentable enough to wear in his presence.' I said I didn't want a brand-new soul, either. I wanted to make my own like Keats did. He said, 'That's spiritual madness.'"

"Look who's talking about madness," I said.

"He makes me feel I'm going mad myself."

"You're the sanest person I know."

"I don't feel very sane these days. Do you think Ricky is schizo?"

"I don't know," I said. "Maybe he has powers we don't."

"Like what?"

"I think there's such a thing as telepathy. There's enough evidence for its existence, even if science can't explain it. Science can't explain gravity, either."

"You think Swami Vijñanananda and Tenzing Rinpoche are communicating with Ricky telepathically?"

"It's possible."

"It sounds crazy."

"Either that or Ricky is." I looked at my watch. "We'd better get going," I said.

You went to the bathroom and I paid the bill.

We took 22 to Interstate 7, which ran north through southern Vermont, and picked up 9 going east at Bennington. There was snow on the mountains and the sky had turned a dirty, slush-colored gray. We had decided to stop for the night in Brattleboro, leaving the last half-hour for the morning. You didn't want to sleep in Keene. "I don't want anyone looking at me and thinking, 'Here's another wicked woman come to kill her child,'" you said. "And not, 'Poor thing, it must be so hard for her,' either. I don't want anyone thinking anything."

The day was the color of wet, cold ashes when we reached Brattleboro. We pulled into a motel outside of town with a vacancy sign. "Should we take one room or two?" I asked.

You were trying to unlock the back of the car and get your bag. "Why doesn't this open?" you asked.

"Because it's a Volkswagen," I said. "That's the engine."

"Well," you said, "if that's where the engine is, how come we were going the other way? I think a double room would be cheaper."

We registered as Mr. and Mrs. John Keats.

The room had a double bed and a chest of drawers with a TV set. There were Gideon's Bibles on the night tables. You went to shower and dress and I lay on the bed and read the eleventh and twelfth chapters of Mark. Then I showered, too, and we drove into Brattleboro. It was a grungy-looking place, with brick factory buildings running down to the Connecticut River beneath a black, starless night. I've been back since and it's been gentrified, with boutique stores and arty cafés and the factories turned into offices and condos, but then we walked through a cheerless New England mill town. All the zest had gone out of us. We had talked all day without thinking about the next day, and the next day was now a night away. We ate in an Italian restaurant with bad food that you hardly touched and drove back to the motel.

We switched on the TV and watched Gregory Peck in *Duel in the Sun* until you said you had seen enough. We switched it off and lay in the half-light coming from the bathroom door. You said, "Hoo, hold me. I'm cold."

I moved over. You nestled against me and I slipped my arm around your shoulder and you rested your head on my chest. "I'm scared," you said.

"You'll be fine," I said. "It's a routine procedure. Hospitals do it all the time."

"This isn't a hospital," you said. "It's the office of a country doctor. The surgical assistant will be his wife and the local vet will do the anesthesia. I'll be their two-uddered cow."

"He must have done a thousand D&C's," I said. "Cindy said he's reliable."

"All kinds of things can go wrong. I could bleed to death or die of septicemia."

"You'll be fine."

"They could perforate my uterus."

"You'll be fine."

"They're going to pry me open with a metal rod and scrape me out with a kitchen spoon. It's like scraping a dish into a garbage pail."

"It's called a curette."

"They'll scrape my baby into the garbage."

You were crying.

"Shhh," I said. "Everything will be all right."

"It's my baby, Hoo."

"I know," I said.

"No, you don't," you said.

I held you tight to keep your sobs from breaking loose and escaping into the dark, starless night.

"Oh please, God," you said.

"Shhh," I said. "Shhh."

"Please."

"You'll be fine."

After a while, you stopped shaking and lay still. You said:

"Maybe I should have the baby."

"How?"

"I'll call the doctor in the morning and cancel."

"You'll marry Ricky?"

"No."

"You can't bring up a child by yourself."

"I'll marry you."

"Me?"

"We'll bring it up together. You'll be a wonderful father."

For a moment, before my anger shot me down, I soared.

"I'm honored, Mellie," I said. "It's a great idea. But let's do it some other time, okay? When it's not just to give my name to Ricky's bhodisattva."

You winced in my arms.

"Look," I said. "I didn't mean that. It was a stupid thing to say. But it is his child."

"It's a tiny little thing. You'll be its father from the time it's no bigger than your thumb. It already has a heart. It has a brain. It has hands with fingers."

"Don't, Mellie," I said. "You'll just torture yourself."

"It has toes. It can wriggle them."

"Don't."

"Little toes, Hoo."

"Stop it," I said.

You rose to get a tissue and sat on the bed and blew your nose. Then you went to the bathroom and came back in a cotton nightgown with red and white roses on it. "I'm sorry," you said. "I didn't think this would happen. I didn't mean to become a weeping womb in front of you."

You took out an alarm clock from your bag and set it for six-thirty. "Go put on your pajamas and come to bed," you said.

"I don't have pajamas," I said. "I never wear them."

"How do you sleep?"

"Naked."

"Is that how you were planning to sleep tonight?"

"How should I sleep?"

"In your underpants."

I went to the bathroom and came back in my underpants and got into bed. You lay in my arms and we fell asleep.

★

Your pale, pale face.

Your dark, dark hair.

The white sheet. Red and white roses.

You opened your eyes. "Is it over?" you asked.

"Yes," I said. "You're fine."

"How long have I been here?"

"About an hour."

"My lips are dry."

I went to the bathroom, wet a washcloth, and ran it over your lips. You shut your eyes and slept. You opened them. "Where am I?" you asked.

"In the recovery room," I said.

Morning sunlight shattered against the window pane. I drew the curtain to keep the slivers from your eyes.

"Is it over?" you asked.

"Yes."

"Wet my lips."

I squeezed the water left in the washcloth onto a finger and ran it over your lips. You sucked my finger like a nursing baby.

"Was it a boy or a girl?"

"I didn't ask," I said. "It's best not to know."

You made more sucking movements with your lips. I wet them and you fell asleep again.

On the ride back to New York, you lay in the back of the car with your knees up. Beneath you I spread the *Manchester Union Leader* to keep you from staining the seat.

You slept most of the way. Your insides hurt despite the painkiller. As we neared the city, you said:

"I'll tell Ricky I had food poisoning."

"From what?"

"My aunt's pickled salmon. We kept running to the bathroom all night. In the morning, the house was like an infirmary."

We both were good liars. That's why we always tried so hard to tell each other the truth. We both knew how easy it was not to.

★

You waited until Ricky was away for the day and told him you had miscarried. Cindy, you said, had gone with you to your gynecologist, who examined you and said you were all right. He told you to rest, and you were already feeling better.

"How did Ricky take it?" I asked.

"Better than I expected," you said. "He's been very caring. He insists on doing all the shopping and cooking. I keep telling him I'm fine and he keeps making me lie down."

But the next time we spoke on the phone that had changed. Ricky was in an agitated state. The voices were more frequent. They were no longer just Swami Vijñanananda and Tenzeng Rinpoche's. "They talk to him all the time," you said. "They talk about the baby."

"What do they say?"

"Horrible things."

"What?"

"Ricky says they're the voices of hungry demons. They say they killed the baby because he put off his chöd ceremony."

"His chair ceremony?"

"It's this Tibetan ritual he's been practicing. You pick some scary or dangerous place, like a forest or haunted house, and you spend a night there. You chant and dance and invite the demons to feast on your body. It's supposed to demonstrate your love for all sentient beings, or something like that."

"Where is he going to find a haunted house?"

"He's decided on Central Park."

"A wise choice," I said. "He'll have plenty of demons."

Just that week, a twenty-four-year-old woman had been murdered in the Ramble. She was out jogging at an hour when more sensible souls were having dinner and was dragged into the bushes, raped, and strangled with her bra strap.

You phoned again a night or two later. You sounded distraught. "He's going to do it tonight," you said. "You've got to stop him, Hoo. He won't listen to me."

I came right over. Ricky was kneeling on your Navaho rug, trying to fit a folded tent into a backpack. On the table were some poles and stakes, a hammer, a coil of rope, a Tibetan bell, a two-headed drum, a piece of burnished bone with a mouthpiece, a wooden staff carved with heads, and a skull-handled dagger.

"Who's going camping?" I asked.

"The tent's part of the ritual," you said. "It's to make the demons comfy."

Ricky ignored you. "As long as you're here, Arjuna," he said, "lend me a hand with this."

"What's it all for?" I asked.

"Mellie will tell you."

"Why don't you?"

"Look, pal," Ricky said, "what it's for is my business. Just help me with this tent."

I picked up the bone instrument. "What's this?"

"A *kangling*. You were sent by Swami Vijñanananda, weren't you?"

"No," I said. "I've never had the pleasure of meeting him."

"He put you up to this."

"And this?" I picked up the staff.

"A *khatvanga*. Put it down."

"That's a neat-looking dagger."

"Put it down." He finished wrestling the tent into the backpack.

"Mellie tells me your ceremony should be in a forest," I said. "Why don't I take you to a real one? I'll borrow Dunk Eldridge's car."

"Tell Swami Vijñanananda to lay off," Ricky said. "I love the man, I really do, but he shouldn't have involved you in this. Stay out of it."

He packed the rest of the things and went to the bedroom.

"Do something," you said.

"What?" I asked. "All I can do is go with him."

"He won't let you."

"I'll follow him. He won't know I'm there."

"Then I'll have to worry about you both."

"What's there to worry about? We've got a dagger for protection and a horn to call for help."

"Hoo, be careful."

Ricky came back from the bedroom in a robe like Tenzeng Rinpoche's.

"Help me on with the pack, Arjuna," he said.

I held the heavy backpack while he slipped his arms through the straps. We waited with him for the elevator. He stepped into it and you said "This is crazy" and I said "What makes you say that?" and ran for the stairs. By the time the elevator door had shut, I had a two-flight lead. I reached the ground floor as the door finished opening and waited for Ricky to leave the lobby before starting after him.

He headed east on 106th Street, a young man in a thin Tibetan robe on a chilly spring night, a pack on his back and sandals on his sockless feet. People stared. It was 1965. There wasn't yet a freak on every New York street corner in those days.

He entered the park opposite a building on Central Park West that looked like a French chateau. I took off my shoes to muffle my footsteps and carried them, keeping as far behind him as I could. He knew where he was going – up a long flight of steps that climbed a granite hill, across some tennis and volleyball courts, and down a winding path on the hill's other side to the bottoms south of the skating rink. A stream clogged with tree limbs and debris trickled through them. Near where it split in two, he crossed it on a wooden footbridge and followed one branch of it over some grassy turf to a dark outcrop of rock, from which it emerged as though from a cave of Pan.

I let him circle the rock and scrambled up it on all fours. From the top, lying on my stomach with my chin propped on one arm, I had a good view. Ricky had gone another twenty yards and stopped beneath a tree. He took off his pack and emptied its contents, placing the tent on the ground and arranging the other things beside it. Then, slipping the dagger into the belt of his robe, he sat down with his back to me.

Several minutes went by. He appeared to be meditating

Central Park was deserted. The only sounds were the growl of distant traffic. It was an hour when people were home but not in bed and all the windows of the big apartment buildings facing the park were lit. Beyond the glittering wall of 59th Street rose the skyscrapers – the Sherry Netherland, the Empire State Building, the Chrysler Building. The sky above them had the violet glow that was the nearest to night a New York sky ever got. The black schist of the rock was sown with silver sparkles.

A cry startled me. Ricky had gotten to his feet and shouted something, a single syllable like "Pah!" He raised the horn to his lips and blew. It sounded like a creaky old door.

He lowered the horn and began to chant. Still chanting, he moved away from me across the grassy turf, in the direction of Fifth Avenue. Pivoting slowly on one foot, he swept the opposite arm near the ground as if bending to retrieve a fallen object and repeated the motion on the other foot.

It was and wasn't a dance. So, once, he had run at me with a football, offering his hips and taking them back as I tagged empty air.

He continued a ways, then traced a circle with his steps and stood in the middle of it. Violently, he stamped his feet. He stamped over and over, chanting more loudly. "Pah!" he shouted. He stopped stamping and scanned the darkness as if to see if anyone had arrived. He raised the horn to his lips and blew.

Was he trampling inky passions? Inviting the demons to the feast? I had no idea what any of it meant. I had no idea what I would do if uninvited guests turned up.

He retraced his steps to the tree. He put down the horn and picked up the drum. Facing 59th Street, he repeated the dance. This time, the space he marked off was three-sided. He stood and stamped, rattling the drum. "Pah!" he shouted. The little balls beat against the drumheads. He shouted at the darkness and peered into it.

He returned to the tree. He put down the drum and picked up the bell. Holding it, he danced straight toward me. I hugged the rock. At its foot, he traced a long arc. Standing midway on it, he stamped and chanted. "Chim sa chim!" he called. "Tro lo lo! Hung hung hung!" The little bell rang in the night.

A bat swooped low. Ricky gave a start and threw up a hand in front of him. "Pah!" he shouted. He drew his dagger and faced the night. "Pah!"

The night was caught on the point of the dagger. He kept it impaled there until the bat was gone.

He returned to the tree and put down the bell. He took the staff and danced toward 110th Street, marking off a square.

The city was a thousand-headed monster, each head glaring with a thousand eyes. He shook his staff at it and stamped.

Chim sa chim! Chim sa chim!

He returned to the tree and danced around it, stamping. Chim sa chim!

He opened the tent. Driving an aluminum pole into the grassy turf, he fitted a grommet of the tent top onto it. Then he did the same with a second pole.

Chanting, he pounded four iron stakes into the ground. He cut lengths of cord with his dagger and fastened the corners of the tent to the stakes.

The tent was standing. He knelt before it, threw down the dagger, and opened his robe, baring his chest to the night.

Chest bared, he chanted. He was offering himself to the demons. He was telling them he wasn't afraid. They could peck out his eyes, gorge on his innards, suck the marrow from his bones, chew on his cartilage and gristle. They could feed on him like vultures.

The thousand-headed monster of the city cradled him in its lap.

The chant was over. On his knees, Ricky backed into the tent. It looked just high enough to sit in. The feast, so it seemed, would take place there.

I kept watch over him for another hour. Most of the lights in the windows had gone out. No sounds came from the tent. Whatever terrors the night still held in store for him, dismembered and devoured by ravenous spirits so that he might rise whole in the morning, the human predators who had kept away so far would not be drawn to him now. I put on my shoes and headed home, stopping by your apartment.

I rang the bell. I had to wait before I heard footsteps. "It's me," I said.

You opened the door in your nightgown.

"He's okay," I said. "He's in the tent with his demons. No one's going to crash their party at this hour."

You shut your eyes and let out a breath. For a moment, I thought you were going to topple backwards and reached out to steady you, but you fell into my arms, smelling of sleep, and I

81

stiffened against you as I did that day in the waves at Coney Island.

The bedroom was too far away. We made love on the Navaho rug. I came quickly. All those years spilled out of me at once.

You put your arms around me and I carried you to the bed and came into you again. Every part of me fit a part of you. Wondrous, we lay thrown together on the shore.

"Mellie," I said.

I still was in you.

"What?"

"This is where I always want to be."

"Don't ever leave me again," you said.

"I never left you a first time."

"Yes, you did," you said. "You did. You did. You did. You did. You did."

"I won't any more," I said.

★

"Hoo," you said. "Wake up."

It was morning. We had been sleeping for hours.

"I'd better go," I said.

You said, "I'll make you coffee while you dress."

"There's no time for that," I said. "Where are my clothes?"

In the end, I found everything but one sock. You offered me a pair of Ricky's.

"One sock is plenty," I said. "Just don't let him find the other."

"Do you love me?" you asked.

"I've always loved you," I said.

"Since when?"

"Since Tripoli."

The elevator came. When the door opened on the ground floor, someone was waiting.

It was Ricky. He was without his pack. His robe was torn. There was blood on his face and one eye was swollen and shut. His nose looked broken again, shoved to one side.

His stare was empty. Perhaps he mistook me for another demon, like the ones who had mugged him in the park.

4

In clearing out the hall closet before moving to Champaign-Urbana, I came across a box of odds and ends. In it were the sandals Ricky wore to his chöd ceremony. For some reason, we hadn't put them in the cartons of his things that I brought to the Silvermans when he was hospitalized. The newspaper they were wrapped in had a story about the success of local merchants in blocking plans for the construction of a world trade center in lower Manhattan.

I've always had a weakness for old newspapers. Once, in Champaign, you sent me down to the basement to look for the Limoges dishes we had gotten for a wedding present. Half an hour later you found me on the basement floor, reading the papers in which they were packed.

The older the news, the fresher it is. It's not just how little of it we remember. It's how nothing turned out the way we thought it would. Only history is blinder than we were, because it knows the outcome and can imagine no other while we imagined everything except it.

I asked you to marry me in the 96th Street subway station. We had gone to see *Six Characters In Search of An Author* at St. Mark's Playhouse. Ricky's presence lingered in your apartment and we slept at mine after that first night. You asked the first time you walked into it:

"When was a woman last here?"

"It must have been Cora," I said.

"It looks it," you said.

You sent me down for a box of Brillo and two bottles of Mr. Clean, and you put on an old T-shirt of mine and a ripped pair of my jeans and mopped the floor and scrubbed the toilet and the bathtub and the sinks and the refrigerator and the stove. You stripped the bed, and helped me turn the mattress, and took the blankets out to the fire escape and beat them with my broken tennis racket, and bought a Japanese lantern for the bare light bulb on the ceiling and a lavender candle to keep out the smell of the refried olive oil in which the Puerto Rican family next-door cooked all its food. It just didn't keep out the roaches. No matter how often we sprayed, they were back every night. "They're like the Viet Cong," you said. "It's their country."

The train was an express. The next stop was 125th Street. I said:

"I want to marry you."

"We get off here," you said.

"I'll get off if you'll marry me," I said.

"But I already proposed to you," you said. "You turned me down."

"Those were different circumstances."

"The doors are closing."

"Let them close."

"Of course I'll marry you," you said. "It was my idea in the first place."

We set the wedding for autumn, for a night of the full moon. We both had been born under one in the same year, you in May and I in June. "What was I waiting for?" I asked.

"You were slow," you said. "I grabbed a moonbeam and slid down. It was like sliding down a fireman's pole. When I got to the bottom I called, 'Come on, Hoo,' but you couldn't make up your mind. Then clouds covered the moon and you had to wait another month."

"Was that really what happened?" I asked.

"No," you said. "But you were slow."

We found a bright, clean studio apartment in Park West Village. It was on the 14th floor, with a picture window facing north over the park. Below us was the pond into which flowed the stream that Ricky and I crossed on the night of his ceremony. It didn't bother me. I had never lived with so much light or been so happy.

The room was L-shaped, with a kitchenette and a bathroom in the crook of the L. When you had finished arranging all our things, they had the same pleased look they had had in your old place. The bed stood by the wall along the room's long side, with your books at one end and mine at the other. Your round table was on the short side by the window. We both worked there, my big Underwood looking down on your little Olivetti. When it was time to eat, we put the typewriters on the floor, spread a tablecloth, and set it with what I called your eclection of silverware, and you, your *arjunkerie*.

Between the table and the bed stood your rubber plant. All that light did it good. It grew so tall that we had to buy bags of earth and replant it in a bigger pot.

It was practically a tree now. I sat at the table, typing on my Underwood. You were reading on the bed. I saw you through the rubber plant as an animal at the edge of a jungle sees a woman in a lit plantation house. I parted the leaves with padding motions. "Grrrr," I said.

"Grrrrrrrr," you growled back.

I crept through the plant. You bared your teeth and growled again. I batted the book from your hands. I turned you on your stomach and sank my teeth into your neck. You squirmed beneath me, arching your haunches. I pulled down your pants and worked my way into you.

86

We made love like tigers. We made it like gulls, crying out over the waves. We made it like eels, wet and slippery after a shower. We made it like snails, slow and sticky in our own secretions. We made it like moles, burrowing blindly through our dreams until we stumbled on each other in the darkness.

I loved watching you sleep. I was an early riser. I'd make myself a cup of coffee, open the blinds a crack, and sit at the table with a book. All I saw of you, turned to the wall with a pillow pulled over your head against the light, was your bare shoulder, from which the blanket had slipped as if the dawn had begun to undress you and stopped to stare in enchantment. Sometimes I took off my clothes and got back into bed, spooning you with my knees tucked beneath you. (The names we had for how we slept, "spoon" and "foxtrot" and "taking a walk" and "dosey-do." "Let's take a walk," you would say in your sleep, and without waking from mine I turned on my back and took your hand and strolled with you through the night as if it were a field of flowers.) I loved your smell beneath the blankets, milky-warm and grassy-sweet. I lay breathing it, then rose and dressed again and made more coffee and took it to the table and opened my book and sat watching you some more.

I loved watching you dress. The last thing you did was braid your hair. You held the long coil of it in your hand, alive and sinuous, debating which of your colored yarns to slip around its neck like a snake charmer.

I loved watching you make breakfast, popping bread in the toaster while turning the bacon in the frying pan and stirring the cocoa paste in our mugs just in time to catch the milk frothing in the saucepan. I loved watching you cook things I had never eaten – chicken livers sautéed in sherry, calamari with lemon and fennel sauce, quiches, crèmes brulées. Each time I bumped into you in the tiny kitchen you had something for my mouth – a spoonful of gazpacho, a cracker spread with guacamole, a kiss tasting of vinaigrette.

I loved watching you eat. First you arranged your food as neatly as if it were in a divided baby plate, the meat and the vegetables and the salad, everything apart. Then you cut it all into little pieces and arranged it again, this time the way you planned to eat it – a bite of lamb chop next to two bites of asparagus, a forkful of mashed potatoes beside a strip of London broil. You meditated on the flavors as you chewed.

I loved watching you do the dishes. I did them once and wasn't given a second chance because you said I left grease on them. After that I kept you company from the kitchen doorway. I said:

"It's an old male trick, you know."

"What is?"

"Purposely leaving grease stains on the dishes."

"Most men couldn't spot a grease stain under a magnifying glass," you said. "They. . .damn!"

"What's wrong?"

"The sink's stopped up."

"I'll bring the plunger," I said.

The plunger made great, gasping sounds. The water still wouldn't go down.

"You'd better get the super," you said.

I didn't want to get the super. "There's an S-trap under the sink," I said. "That's where the problem has to be. I'll open it."

"Why don't you just get the super, Hoo," you said.

I said, "It's faster to do it myself."

I brought a wrench and a bucket and opened the trap. I didn't slide the bucket beneath the opened trap fast enough and dirty dishwater sloshed onto the floor.

You went to get the mop. I pulled a glob of guck from the trap. "Here's what did it," I said.

You mopped the floor while I screwed the trap back in place. You began to wash the dishes again. The trap fell off and more water poured on the floor.

"Jesus!" you said. "Why didn't you screw that thing on properly?"

I tried screwing it tighter. It jammed on the thread of the drainpipe.

"Fuck!" I said.

"What is it now?"

"It's stuck. I can't work it on and I can't work it off."

"I knew this would happen. You should have gone for the super."

"You shouldn't have let all that crud get past the drain filter."

"Hoo, that has nothing to do with it. You were just too stubborn to ask for help."

"I didn't need help."

"Well, you'd better go get it now."

"Go get it yourself."

"All right," you said. "If you're embarrassed to, I will. Just don't play erector set with my sink again."

"It's my sink too," I said. "And I'll do what I want with it."

"Stop shouting."

You were shouting, too. I walked out and slammed the door without taking the key.

It was our first fight. After the second you know it's not the end of everything, but the first always feels as if it is. I walked the streets block after block, paying no attention to where I was going. I had gotten as far as 72nd and Broadway when I nearly stepped on a tiger.

It was a windup toy. A man with a carton of them had set half a dozen out on the sidewalk. They had little drums strapped to their waists, which they beat with little sticks held in white-gloved hands. As soon as one stopped drumming, the man put another in its place and rewound it. His hands were as busy as the tigers'.

"How much are they?" I asked.

"A buck apiece."

I picked one up. It went on drumming in my hand. It had bowlegs and "Happy Tiger" written on its drum, but its eyes didn't look happy at all. They looked as though it had been crying.

I paid a dollar and walked back with Happy Tiger. Maybe I ran. I wound it and rang the bell and waited for you to open the door.

"Who is it?" a woman asked.

It wasn't your voice, even though the door said 14T.

"Who are you?" I asked.

"Who are *you*?" I could hear the fear rising in her as fast as it was rising in me.

"I live here," I said. "What are you doing in my apartment? Where is Mellie?"

"*I* live here," she said. "There is no Milly. Go away. Go away or I'll call the police."

"Where's Mellie?" I screamed. "What did you do with her?"

"I'm calling the police."

I thought I was going mad. I thought I had gone mad. I hoped I had gone mad, because if I hadn't, you didn't exist.

I rode the elevator back down and rushed out of the building. I would have gone mad in one more second if I hadn't glanced up at the number on the awning.

It was 392.

We lived in 400.

90

There were four buildings in Park West Village, all looking exactly alike. I didn't know they had the same interiors, too: the same lobbies, the same elevators, the same hallways, the same apartments. In my hurry to give you Happy Tiger, I had walked into the wrong building.

I ran to 400. I took the elevator to our floor and rang the bell. You opened the door.

Happy Tiger beat his drum.

"Grrrrrrrr," you said.

★

We had to tell Ricky. You wanted me to do it. You had been to see him in the hospital after he was committed and didn't want to go again. He wasn't coherent. He was in terror of being attacked again. He wouldn't open his swollen eye because he was sure it had been eaten. The doctors were thinking of electric shock treatment.

I suggested going together.

"That would only make it worse for him," you said.

"All right," I said. "I'll go."

I took the subway to Union Turnpike and a bus to 263rd Street and walked the two blocks from there to the entrance of the hospital. At the gate I was told that Richard Silverman was now in Lowenstein 2. I had to skirt a parking lot and follow a concrete path to get there.

There were three brick Lowensteins along one side of what resembled a college quad. It was a Sunday and people were sprawled on the lawn. You couldn't always tell the patients from the visitors. On the wall of Lowenstein 2 someone had scrawled in chalk, TIRED OF LIVING? TRY THE HILLSIDE REST CURE.

I asked for Ricky at the nurses' station. "He's in Room 6," a

91

nurse said. But the only occupant in Room 6 was a young man in pajamas sitting on a bed. "Hi," he said. "If you're looking for someone, that person might be someone else."

Back in the lobby, I saw Ricky trying to work a candy machine.

"It's all out of Almond Joys," he said. Although his face had healed and both eyes were wide open, he had a puffy look.

We went to sit on the lawn. He walked slowly and I had to shorten my stride to match his. We found an empty patch of grass and sat down.

"How are you doing?" I asked.

"Pretty good," he said. "Pretty good. My parents always wanted me to be in an Ivy League atmosphere."

"You've put on weight."

"That's the Thorazine. It's full of calories."

"You'll be out of here soon," I said.

"Sure," he said. "As soon as they find a way to take out the radio."

At one end of the lawn, two young men were tossing a football.

"That's the problem. It's too big to fit through my skull. It was picking up the whole fucking universe."

"You're still hearing voices?"

"No, man. They zapped the tubes. Now there's just static all the time. It's driving me nuts. They'll figure it out, though. They've got seven doctors working on my case."

Back and forth the ball went in long spinning arcs. It was a warm September day. The chimneys of the hospital's power unit sent lazy smoke into the sky.

"Mellie and I are getting married," I said.

"You and Mellie?" He frowned as if trying to recall who that was.

"We wanted you to know."

"Sure thing," he said. "I appreciate that."

"I . . . ." I hadn't planned how to say it. "I want you to know there was nothing between us — I mean nothing romantic — before all this happened."

He waved a hand. "She's a great girl, Mellie. I always thought you two were meant for each other. You should have fucked her back in high school before I did."

It was the only allusion made by either of us, if that's what it was, to meeting by the elevator that night.

"When is the wedding?" he asked.

"Next month," I said. "October 2. You're invited."

"Great," he said. "I'll have my secretary make a note of it."

It was the last time I saw him.

★

The day before our wedding I wrote you a letter. I wrote:

Mellie,

When we were in high school, I thought one life would not be enough for me. I wanted to do a million things, to love a million women. I wanted to live a thousand lives.

Now even a thousand seem too few. Not because I still want to love a million women, but because I want to love you a million times.

If we had only one life to live together, I would live it with you joyfully, although I would wish for more. If we had ten lives, or a hundred lives, I would still wish for more. If you and I could be born over and over, I would wish it always to be as you and me, so that each time we could be together again. If after a thousand lives with you I

93

was told I was living the last one, I would feel cheated. But if I had to choose between one life with you or a thousand without you, I would choose that one no matter how short it was. I would choose it now and always.

Hoo

★

On the morning of our wedding, I bought you a present. I saw it in the window of a custom jewelry store on Amsterdam Avenue when I went to have my hair cut. It was an enameled locket on which was an angel with flowing hair and spread wings and the inscription *àngel de la guardia*. I bought a gold chain to go with it and stopped at a grocery for a carton of milk. On the magazine rack by the check-out counter were some astrology booklets. I took one and turned to Gemini. The prediction for October 2 was, "Something will happen today to change your life."

They never said things like that, those fortune-cookie horoscopes. They always hedged their bets.

That was the first sign and wonder of our wedding day.

I took a square of paper from a memo pad, wrote on it in small letters

> Melisande! What are dreams?
> What is death? A vain to-do.
> The truth belongs to love alone,
> And, always fair one, I love you,

folded it, and slipped it into the locket. Then I put the locket in my pants pocket and went for a walk.

It was my last walk before being your husband and each step felt like a word in a prayer. A moist breeze was blowing; the

94

forecast was for rain later in the day. I crossed the park, cutting across the baseball diamonds, and came out on Fifth Avenue, just north of the Metropolitan. I walked another block and started down Madison, looking at the shop windows. A voice called:

"Hoo!"

You were leaning out the window of a slowly moving bus.

"Get off at the next stop!" I shouted.

I ran to the stop. You were just getting off. You were carrying a bag with your wedding dress and were on your way to pick up the baby orchids for your hair.

"I can't believe it," you said.

"Do you know what the odds against this are?" I asked.

"It's a sign," you said. "It's a sign we'll always find each other."

I made you shut your eyes and hung the locket around your neck and fastened it.

That was the second sign and wonder of our wedding day.

It rained that night. It was still raining when we stepped into the street from our wedding.

"Look," you said.

You tilted the umbrella someone had given you. Rain fell on the shawl you had wrapped around your wedding dress.

Above us, the clouds had parted and the full moon had come into view.

"It's a moon shower," you said.

"I've never seen a moon shower," I said.

"Neither have I," you said.

That was the third sign and wonder of our wedding day.

★

We drove up to Vermont for our honeymoon. Friends of my parents lent us their cabin on a pond near Wilmington.

Dunk let us have his VW. By now the floor shift and I got along well.

The cabin was musty. The pantry was empty except for a bag of salt and some jars of spices, and there was no cooking gas left for the stove. But there was a good smell of wood, and of pine cones heaped in a basket by the fireplace, and of fires that the ashes still remembered. We opened the windows and drove to a supermarket in Wilmington, and we bought steaks to grill and potatoes to roast in a fire, and cucumbers and tomatoes and onions and lemons and olive oil and vinegar, and bread and jam and coffee and sugar and wine and milk and butter, and a salami and a can of sardines and mustard and mayonnaise, and matches and toilet paper and aluminum foil and paper toweling and garbage bags and candles and a plastic container. We drove back with it all and brought in wood from the woodpile and gathered kindling. I crumpled toweling in the fireplace and scattered pine cones on it and laid the kindling on the pine cones and wood on the kindling. Then we put the milk and butter in the container and wedged it in shallow water between a rock and a post of the wooden dock running into the pond. Ducks drifted on the water at the dock's end.

The sun was hot. The water was cool. "Let's go for a swim," I said.

You said, "It'll be freezing further out."

"We'll wade in and see," I said.

We took off our clothes. You left on your *ángel de la guardia*. I saw the pond tremble at your splendor.

We waded into the water. It grew colder by the step. When you were up to your knees, you decided you had gone far enough.

"Let's sit on the dock," I said.

We walked to the end of it. I put my arms around you and

kissed you. Your skin was warm from the sun. "Mellie, we're jumping," I said.

You screamed as we hit the freezing water. The ducks took off in a fright. I let go of you and shouted, "I'll race you to the cabin."

"I'll kill you when we get there," you said.

We splashed to the shore. I reached the cabin first and grabbed a towel. Your teeth were chattering. I dried you and undid your braid and dried your long hair, and then I handed you the towel and you dried me. I lit the paper toweling and a fire blazed up. I spread a blanket in front of it and we lay down.

"Now kill me," I said.

When we woke, the fire had gone out and the cabin was in shadow. We dressed and went outside and watched the sun drop behind the pond. The autumn trees were reflected in it. They grew upside-down, their shimmering trunks descending to their branches. You said:

"It's a fairy world. Do you think there are still nymphs and water sprites down there?"

"It's easy to see why people once believed in them," I said.

"Yes," you said. "They were young and foolish. Now even the water sprites are old and wise. They look up at the reflection of the trees in the sky and they say, 'It's easy to see why we once believed in earthlings.'"

"When we were in high school," I said, "Ricky told me that once, in third or fourth grade, he was looking out the window and suddenly he wondered, how did he know he wasn't dreaming everything he saw? Maybe there was no one else beside him and it would all disappear when he woke up."

"And leave not a rack behind," you said.

"Is that Keats?"

"No. *The Tempest*."

97

"I told him I'd had a thought like that, too. Only what I thought was: suppose someone is dreaming me and *he* wakes up."

"Were you scared?" you asked.

"A little," I said. "Wouldn't you have been?"

"Yes," you said. "But I would have been more scared if I had been Ricky."

"That time I walked into 392 by mistake," I said, "I thought that's what had happened. I thought I had dreamed you – that I had dreamed my whole life – and that I had been woken by our argument."

"It must have been awful."

"It was worse than that."

"That's what I meant," you said. "If someone wakes from dreaming us, at least we'll disappear together."

★

From the pages of Sir James Frazer's *Golden Bough*:

Hoo,

I won't be home for lunch. There's egg salad in the refrigerator. Don't forget we're going to the movies with Rob & Cindy tonight.

m.

What movie was that? What movies did we see in those years? *The Appaloosa, Bonnie and Clyde, Alice's Restaurant, Easy Rider, Zabriskie Point, A Man and A Woman,* Bergman's *Persona,* Bergman's *Hour of The Wolf, A Night at the Opera, Casablanca* and *The Maltese Falcon* in a Bogart festival, the whole *Apu Trilogy* in a single day at the Thalia – plus all the ones I've forgotten. I don't remember going to any of them with Rob and Cindy.

I once read about an old Jewish custom of not destroying any writing with God's name on it, even if it was only an invocation of his blessing at the top of a letter or note, even if it was just an epithet for him. Every such scrap of paper was consigned to a special storage room.

Even if it was just his initial.

★

From the paperback of Bellow's *Herzog*:

> Hoo,
>   On your way home, take out some cash from the
> bank.
>   m.

★

From *The Collected Poems of W. B. Yeats* (my copy):

⌄

I've gone to bed. Spoon me.

I've gone to bed. Spoon me.

You once asked:
"If you couldn't be human, what would you most like to be?"
"A seagull," I said. "What would you?"
"A flower," you said.

★

From my *Oxford Universal Dictionary*, pp. 620–1 (Envoy–Epicureanism):

Hoo,

    Jerry Lauder phoned. I said you'd call back.

m.

I haven't a clue who that was.

★

From my Bekker Aristotle, Book VII of the *Physics*:

Hoo,

    Gifford changed our meeting from 3 to 5, so I won't be back before 6:30. Wish me luck!

m.

You came home practically in tears.

"He wants me to rewrite it," you said.

"Why?"

You threw your thesis on a chair. Pages slipped to the floor. I bent to pick them up. You said:

"Leave them there, I'll dump them down the incinerator chute later."

"Just take a deep breath and tell me about it," I said.

"There's nothing to tell. He wants me to rewrite it. I'm not going to."

"What does he want you to rewrite?"

"The whole second half. The soul-making part. He says I should stick to the poem."

"You have stuck to the poem. You've read it more deeply than anyone before you."

"He thinks I'm over my head. If he had his way, I'd just grind it up and can it with a label that said, 'Contains paradoxes, ironies, tensions, ambiguities, and one hundred per-cent pure formal analysis with no harmful additives.'"

"You'll work something out with him."

"I won't work out anything. I've had it."

"What does that mean?"

"I'm quitting school."

"That's not a decision to make just like that," I said.

"I've made it," you said.

You picked the pages off the floor, added them to those on the chair, and headed for the door.

I blocked your way.

"Sit down," I said. "I'm not letting you throw away a year's work."

"Yesterday I was reading the letters," you said. "The last ones from Italy. He knew he was dying. He wrote Fanny's mother from Naples, 'If ever a person was born without the faculty of hoping, I am he.' He writes Brown that all the keepsakes Fanny has given him are torture, because he knows he'll never see her again. He says a letter from her would be more than he could bear. He was younger than we are, Hoo. He was twenty-five years old."

You sat on the floor like a mourner. "I should have been there," you said.

"Where?"

"With him in Rome."

"That might have been difficult to arrange."

"He had Severn. Severn was devoted, but he wasn't what he needed. He made him ride through Rome on a pony. Just think of it, Hoo! He's dying – he's spitting arterial blood – and he has to ride a pony through the streets every day because the doctor thinks he needs exercise. I'd never have let him do it, all slumped in the saddle like a prisoner led to the gallows."

"You're right," I said. "You should have been there. You would have made him chicken soup."

"With Trude's matzo balls."

I kissed you. "Do you know what your lips are like when you smile after you've been crying?"

"What?"

"A rainbow," I said.

But you went ahead with it. "What will you do now?" I asked after you told Gifford and informed the bursar's office.

"Sleep late tomorrow," you said.

"No, really."

"I don't know," you said. "Maybe learn to weave."

I must have looked doubtful.

"Don't make such a face. It's something I've always wanted to do. I'm tired of words."

"You might as well be tired of breathing."

"Breathing is being alive. Writing articles on 'Antinomy and Antiphony in Keats' *Endymion*' isn't. Right now I can't think of anything I'd like better than sitting quietly on a stool putting colors together."

You signed up for a weaving course at Riverside Church.

★

From Gildersleeve & Lodge's *Latin Grammar* (the revised and enlarged third edition):

If you boil water, use a pot. There's bleach in the kettle.

m.

★

From Wittgenstein's *Philosophical Investigations*, in red ink:

∨‾

I felt your prick in me all day. I feel anointed by you.

❧

*

From Bourciez's *Éléments de Linguistique Romane*:

Hoo,
    I'm having lunch with Cindy. Take the lamb chops out
of the freezer.
        m.

*

From *Procli Commentarium in Parmenidem, pars ultima adhuc inedita, interprete Guillemo de Moerbeke*:

Hoo,
    The mattress is being delivered today. Be sure to stay
home until it comes.
        m.

I don't remember buying a new mattress. It couldn't have been later than 1969, because I never looked at de Moerbeke after my defense until, not long ago, I needed to check something there. Your note fell out of Proclus' discussion of rest and motion in Book II. My dissertation's reconstruction of the lost Greek text at the end of Book VII on the basis of de Moerbeke's thirteenth-century Latin translation was more ambitious than it needed to be, especially since he was working with a manuscript different from the extant ones. But his translation had been published for the first time in the 1950s by Kablansky and was still virgin territory, and I picked an obvious aspect of it to work on. By the time I realized I could have chosen something simpler, it was too late to turn back.

You never shared my affinity for the Neoplatonists. You didn't think we had slid down a moonbeam. Neither did I. But the feeling of a somewhere I had been in or come from often haunted me when I was young. Stung by a childhood injustice, or confused by a response to beauty so strong that it felt like a prodding in the pit of my stomach, I would think I dimly remembered a place where Justice had reigned and Beauty had been in all things. When I first read Plato in high school, his theory of recollection made perfect sense to me.

But I also had the feeling of having been *here* before. I had frequent déjà vus. They occurred without warning, leaving me as dizzy as if I had looked down into a chasm. Although they happened in perfectly ordinary situations – riding the bus to school, coming home from the park with a baseball bat on my shoulder, eating the same breakfast I ate every morning – they had details whose familiarity jolted me with the knowledge that I hadn't witnessed them in this life: the little girl saying to her friend "I wish I had shoes like yours," the sudden shadow cast by a cloud at the very moment that a bird called from the branch of a tree, the blue and white checked tablecloth on which four smudges of cereal formed a diamond in a puddle of milk.

As I grew older, these experiences became less common and eventually stopped. I haven't had one in years. I suppose Wordsworth would have taken this as proof that our birth is but a sleep and a forgetting.

When three universities offered me a teaching job, Illinois seemed the best bet. It wasn't Berkeley or Princeton, and it was known more for its engineering school than its humanities, but it was an academically respectable place and had one of the best Classics libraries in the country.

"And it's right near Chicago," you said. "We can drive there for concerts and plays. I'll take you to my favorite spots."

"It doesn't look so near," I said. A Rand McNally atlas lay opened on my knees.

"It is," you said. "It's just a few inches away."

Anyway, it would be only a pit stop. I'd publish and get an assistant professorship somewhere else. Meanwhile, we'd have a house with a garden and enough space for a study for me and a workroom for you.

"And a dog," I said. "A Dalmatian."

"An Irish setter."

"Both."

"And babies."

"How many?"

"Six."

"*Six*?"

"Seven. One for each day of the week."

"'Tuesday!' I said. "'Stop pulling Wednesday's hair and behave yourself.' Ouch!"

You were pulling my hair and kissing me all over.

*

From Hans Jonas' *The Gnostic Religion*:

Ego sum fera super te!

From Volume II of the twelve-volume 1791 edition of Gibbon's *Decline and Fall* that you gave me:

My great, great love,
    Happy Birthday! If life is the Grand Prix, this year was the best lap yet.

We celebrated our birthdays together, whenever the moon between them was full. I gave you pearl earrings. You gave me the Gibbon and a wind-up monkey driving a race car. I put it next to Happy Tiger.

★

From Philo's Περὶ Ἀφθαρσίας Κόσμου:

Hoo,
    I went for my appointment at the gynecologist's. Let's eat out tonight, ok?
                    m.

You had decided to go off the pill.
I didn't see what the hurry was.
"There isn't any," you said. "I just wanted to be pregnant when we moved."
"What if you're not? So we won't have a Made in New York baby. That's a handicap it will have to learn to live with."
"I don't care where it's made," you said. "I'd just like it to be born next spring."
"Why next spring?"

"Spring's a nice time to be born."

"If you're a calf."

"Back in April," you said, "I was looking at the new leaves on the trees. They come pushing out from their buds like little fingers. I thought. . . ."

I didn't ask what you had thought.

We moved at the end of August. The fall semester started in late September.

★

From *The Aeniad*:

Hoo,

I tried getting hold of you, but the department secretary didn't know where your Humanities section met. Ricky killed himself yesterday. Ralph Silverman called. The funeral is at 3 at Mt. Lebanon Cemetery in Queens. I'm leaving now for Riverside Chapel. I expect I can get a ride to the cemetery. If you can make it, take a taxi.

m.

I took a taxi and got there as dirt was being shoveled on the coffin. There weren't many people: you, Rob and Cindy, Linda and Moysh, the Silvermans, a few of their friends, Ricky's psychiatrist from Hillside, and two or three bashful men who had worked with Ricky in the bakery he found a job in after his release. He must have been very lonely that last year.

"How did he do it?" I whispered.

"He jumped out a window," you said.

Phil Donati, who had been in the Party with the Silvermans, spoke briefly. He hadn't seen Ricky in years, he said, but he remembered him as a teenager, a bright, handsome young man with a friendly smile and a deep concern for the downtrodden and oppressed. Not just his family and friends, but the whole world, in which he might have done so much, was the poorer for losing him.

The psychiatrist spoke, too. He had only known Ricky in the few months he had been in Hillside. Although it was unfair to judge anyone on that basis, he said, Ricky was one of the most intelligent patients he had ever treated, with a wry sense of humor about his own condition. He remembered one thing in particular that Ricky had said to him. They were talking about schizophrenia and Ricky said, "Dr. Krulevich, you psychiatrists are so interested in the voices people hear. What about all the ones they don't hear?"

Dr. Krulevich said:

"That made a great impression. There are too many voices we don't hear. Ricky's own voice won't be heard any more. It was unique and we'll miss it."

You whispered:

"Hoo! You should say something."

"A window where?" I asked.

"At his parents'. Say something."

"There's nothing to say," I said.

We rode back to Manhattan with the Donatis. "How are Ralph and Tillie coping?" I asked.

"They're crushed," said Phil Donati. "Ricky was everything for them. You should go see them. They'd be grateful."

"I will," I said.

I never did. Years later I saw Ralph Silverman standing on a street corner, waiting for the light to change. Before I could make up my mind what to do, it had changed and he was no longer there.

There are big things one regrets and there are little things. The little things can seem less forgivable, because it would have been easier to do them differently. I don't know whether it would have given Ralph pleasure had I gone over and said something about Ricky or whether it would have caused him pain by reminding him of what — perhaps only for a minute, perhaps for an hour or a day — he had managed to forget. I only know I should have done it.

5

He had just told the Pharisees to render to Caesar what was Caesar's when there came to him the Sadducees, which say there is no resurrection. And they asked him, saying:

Master, Moses wrote us that if a man's brother die and leave his wife behind him and leave no children, his brother should take his wife and raise up seed unto his brother.

Now there were seven brethren. And the first took a wife, and dying left no seed.

And the second took her and died, neither left he any seed. And the third likewise.

And the seven had her and left no seed. Last of all, the woman died also.

In the resurrection, therefore, when they shall rise, whose wife shall she be of them? For the seven had her to wife.

One might credit them with a sense of humor, the Sadducees. After all, two brothers would have been quite enough.

But in fact there were seven. The last, born long after the others, was an infant when she wed the first.

He was actually the third. The eldest, a grain merchant, was married and the next eldest had left home, it was said, for the countries of the sea. She had no idea where those countries might be. She lived in a large village in the Galilee – some thought it deserved to be called a town – and had never seen the sea.

She was sixteen. He was three years older. The match was arranged by their parents. She was the beauty of the village, with long-lashed eyes the color of dark jasper. His father paid a large bride-price for her. Having grown up dominated by his older brothers, he was worried by his good fortune, as well might be anyone coming into possession of something costly for which he is not properly insured.

On their wedding night, his shyness confused her. She had never kissed a man on the mouth, and when she lifted hers to his, their teeth clashed with a dull ring. She giggled in spite of herself and his passion flagged. Yet in time their embraces grew bolder; new sensations prickled her like the swelling of her breasts the year her childhood had ended. Although the days with him were dull, she looked forward to the nights. Half a year into their marriage, a grindstone being lowered into place in his father's olive press broke loose from its tackle and crushed him. She got through the funeral rites as she had gotten through the wedding rites, doing as she was told. Long afterwards she remembered him, as she remembered herself from that time, dimly but wistfully, more as a first lover than a first husband.

When time passed and it was clear she was not with child, she was called on to wed the fourth brother, a tall fellow with a neck like a camel's who worked in the eldest's grain business. She balked. He was unappealing. Though slow to dawn on her, the advantages of being an attractive young widow without children did not escape her. She glimpsed, as though through a hole in a garden wall, a view of something that, had she been able to give it a name, she might have called a life of her own.

She asked him to release her. At first he agreed. The procedure was simple if crude. He would renounce her before a court of judges and she would pull a shoe from his foot, spit in his face, and proclaim, "Thus shall be done to the man who will not upbuild his brother's house." Then he would hobble off on one shoe and she would be granted her freedom.

But it was not to be. His family was opposed. His father, loathe to write off a large investment, urged him to reconsider. This was not difficult to get him to do. He was of an irresolute nature and knew he could never win such a prize as her unaided. Afraid to face her, he sent a messenger to tell her he had changed his mind.

For weeks after their wedding, she refused to talk to him. Her hostile silence first chastened, then alarmed him. He was contrite. He begged forgiveness. He would do anything to make her happy. She looked at him coldly.

In the end, she relented a bit. His abjectness stirred her pity as it might have been stirred by a lame animal. From time to time, she even let him into her bed. Yet his clumsy claspings repelled her. A camel! She wished he looked more like his red-bearded eldest brother, whose eyes were often on her.

They were hungry, those eyes. Her brother-in-law had three children and his wife's belly was bulging again. Once, when they were alone in the granary, she felt him so close behind her that the hairs on her neck bristled against the chain of her gold pendant.

The next time they were by themselves there, she was counting sacks of wheat while standing in an aisle between two rows of them. He started down it to fetch a wheelbarrow. She did not move aside and his shoulder brushed against her. She held her ground. He seized her. Over and over they rolled in the golden-brown wheat until she was pinned in a pocket of it. The thrusts of his loins were fierce, famished. She met each with one of her own. He, she, he, she: they were wielding a two-handled saw. It took the tree a long time to topple. Who could believe how long it held out, even as it groaned for deliverance? It fell with a shudder that started in the pit of her and traveled all the way to her fingers and her toes.

She lay panting by his side, her lips breaking out in new tremors and her teeth chattering as though she had been pulled from cold, dark water.

The chain of her pendant was torn. She had it fixed by a jeweler. She felt no guilt or sin. She had wanted a life of her own. It had been stolen from her. She had taken it back.

They met often in the granary, bolting the door, their only witness an incurious cat kept to catch mice in the grain. His lust was great. So was hers.

She knew the punishment for adultery. But though she slipped away so often and with such careless excuses that her husband had to suspect something, she also knew he would never accuse her.

Her brother-in-law's wife went into labor. For a day the woman screamed so loudly that it could only have been that the baby inside her had joined its cries to hers. The midwives were unable to save either.

Soon after the week of condolence calls was over, her second husband took his life. He was found hanging from the beams of the granary, a rope around his long neck. He had indeed done all he could to make her happy. Of all her husbands, she was later to reflect, of him alone could this be said.

In the year of mourning that had to pass before she and her brother-in-law could wed, she was scrutinized closely. There were rumors. Some hoped for a red-haired bastard to confirm them. Some claimed she had drunk a potion to get rid of it. No bastard was born.

Her marriage to the eldest brother lasted six years. They

quarreled a lot. Sometimes he hit her. She fought back. He threw her to the floor and took her by force while she struggled beneath him, cursing and biting until the dark waves swept her up. For a day or two, they doted on each other. Then they fought again.

She was a good mother to her husband's small children, two boys and a girl. Sometimes they were joined in play by his youngest brother. She had a way with them. She never treated children less fairly than she treated adults. The difference was that they treated her fairly, too.

She longed for a child of her own. None came. Her husband made light of it. His children were hers, he said. Why did they need more? Any sons born to her would just inherit in his dead brothers' names.

He had no idea of the ache in her womb. It was a void that sucked all into it. All around her women had babies, like the litters of kittens that mewed in the granary. How could something so simple elude only her?

The kittens were drowned. She could have drowned every baby in the village. She could have murdered their mothers, the childhood friends who had once envied her beauty. They sat nursing in little groups, chatting stupidly while the milk dribbled from their breasts.

None of her old friendships was left. The only person in the village she could talk to was the fifth brother. He and she were the same age. He was a scribe, a man who read and copied books. He had once been betrothed to the miller's blond daughter and had come to ask her advice.

She had been flattered. But why did he have doubts about the match? The miller's daughter was full of light.

Yes, he answered gloomily. And her light would get lost in his darkness.

Which, she asked, did he fear for more: her light or his darkness?

Her light, he said.

Then marry her, she told him. Light is stronger than darkness.

He broke the engagement anyway. The miller's daughter married the son of a publican and the scribe remained single. He had a room in the house of his parents, to which he added an outside staircase to give him a private entrance. At night, when the village was dark, a candle burned in the window.

Sometimes, when her husband and his children were asleep, she climbed the stairs to the scribe's room. Strips of parchment lay on a worktable alongside pens and pots of ink and glue. The finished scrolls stood on a shelf, tied with flaxen strings. She wondered what was in them.

All kinds of things, he said. People's thoughts.

About what?

He shrugged. Everything. Life. God.

She too had thoughts about God, she said.

He asked what they were.

She thought, she said, that God should be punished for punishing her.

She expected him to rebuke her. Yet he only said that God was already punished enough.

Her husband died suddenly. She was in the market when someone ran to tell her. He was lying on his back, one hand on his chest and his mouth agape like the mouths of the fish in the market.

His three children were put in the care of their grandparents. Another year of mourning went by. When she walked in the village she now was looked at, not with disapproval, but with fear. She saw a grocer take a fig she had touched to test its ripeness and fling it into the gutter.

Ignore them, the scribe told her. Your soul is purer than any of theirs.

If he could have seen her soul, she thought, he would never have said that.

She was outwardly in the full bloom of life, unmarred by the births that caused the women of the village to go slack by the time they were thirty, their breasts sagging and their hips putting on fat. At most, a tightness of her lips made them look thinner than they were and the two lines that appeared in her forehead when she frowned sometimes forgot to go away. All her beauty had only been a curse.

It was then that the second brother returned. He wore a knee-length Greek cloak fastened with a bronze pin and a rimmed Greek hat like an upside-down bowl. A strapping man with a hearty laugh, even his paunch suggested power, as if the muscles of his chest extended into it.

He had been to lands across the sea that no one had heard of: Lydia, and Cappadocia, and Phrygia, and Colchis, and Thrace. Beyond them lay a second sea that took nine days to cross, into which flowed a river carrying crumbs of gold that were gathered in the fleeces of sheep. Upstream was a lake where lived huge water rats with tails like mats and teeth like ax-blades. Buying their fur from trappers, he had grown rich by shipping it to Calchedon. His wealth now exceeded his father's.

Although no one believed all the second brother's stories, his wealth was real, for he came with expensive gifts. It was now his turn to perform the ceremony of the shoe. Extending a leather boot bought in Athens, he would let her pull it from his foot, spit at him, and sunder herself at last from his family.

However, he was smitten by the sight of her. Retracting the boot she knelt to remove, he declared he would marry her.

There was consternation. He had had more than his share of desirable women, from the wild wives of trappers to the elegant courtesans of Athens. How could he risk his life for a slayer of men and seed?

He, who had studied something called philosophy in the academy of Athens, laughed at such superstition. If it rained three times in a row on the third day of the month, did that mean it would rain then in the fourth month?

She let him convince her. They would travel. She would see the world. She would realize how backward the village was and learn to appreciate her worth. She would have a life she had never dreamed of.

They sailed from Acre. They saw the great lighthouse of Alexandria and took a boat up the Nile to the Pyramids. (So much work, she thought, for such stupid triangles!) They spent the springtime in Rome, renting a villa near the theater of Marcellus. She learned some Latin and conversed in the broken Greek she knew from home. Their new acquaintances found her charming. She saw her beauty glitter in their eyes. The ache in her womb grew duller. Seated in her chamber by her jars of creams, she stared thoughtfully at the mirror on the table.

They set out for Athens in early summer, stopping to see the Pythian games in Delphi and arriving in time for the Mysteries. They had a fine hilltop view of the procession to Eleusis and the dances in the Rharian Field.

In the autumn, plague broke out. She was spared by it. Her husband died in its third week.

It had truly been a year she had never dreamed of.

She now lived in a pillared house inside the Acharnian gate, the widow of a prosperous merchant from Coele-Syria, his business run for her by his chief steward. His Athenian friends adopted her. Invitations to her dinner parties were sought after. She took a lover, a lawyer from the Peloponnese who did funny imitations of his clients and their judges. She exchanged him for a teacher of rhetoric.

The teacher of rhetoric was at the agora when a servant announced that a stranger was at the door. He spoke with a foreign accent and wished to see her.

In the language of the village, which she had not spoken for so long that she was afraid to make mistakes in it, she asked the scribe why he had come.

To marry you, he said.

She looked at him unbelievingly. Did he think the foolish customs of the village still meant anything to her? She had no intention of marrying again. She was happy with the life she had. Four husbands had died on her account. Why make him the fifth?

Because I love you, he said.

No one had ever wanted to marry her for such a reason before. More softly, she asked: since when?

Since always, he said.

Was that, she asked, why he hadn't married the miller's daughter?

Yes, he said. Did she remember what she had told him?

She remembered

Love is stronger than death, he said.

Looking back, she could not decide whether their brief marriage had been the happiest or most miserable time of her life. He was moody. He hated Athens. He detested her friends. She had to attend their entertainments by herself while he stayed in his room writing. She could hear him pacing there. Once she heard a noise and ran to see what it was. He had hurled an inkpot at the words he had written.

Yet when she opened her eyes in the morning and saw him, propped on an elbow, regarding her with wonder, she felt blessed. She had never been looked at that way. He really did see her soul. If he died, no one would know who she was.

Although he was healthy, she lived in fear for him. Each twinge he felt might be the start of a deadly illness. Every goodbye seemed like a final parting. When a letter came from the village in the Galilee with news that the sixth brother, a consumptive, had not long to live, she begged him not to go.

He disregarded her and went anyway. He and his brother had always been close.

She waited to hear news. Time passed and a letter arrived. He had caught his brother's illness and was too weak to travel back to Athens.

She set out for the village at once. He was dead by the time she arrived. The sixth brother, though pale and feverish, was still alive.

The village seemed smaller than she remembered it. From afar, its stone houses resembled piles of rocks. Was this the place some had wanted to call a town?

To her surprise, the villagers treated her with respect. She had ceased to be one of them. She now came from the same great world that had sent its legions to conquer them, its governors to rule them, its tax collectors to plunder them. She spoke its language and wore its clothes. She could no longer be judged by them as they judged themselves.

She visited her fifth husband's grave. After his flesh had rotted, his bones would be exhumed and placed in the family sepulcher. She felt too much rage at him to weep.

That evening the brothers' mother came to her with a request. Once an ample woman, she had shriveled like an olive left on the branch after harvest. She addressed the murderess of her sons with the same deference shown by the villagers.

Her next-to-youngest son was now dying, she said. The doctors gave him no more than a few weeks. He had been sickly all his life and had never known a woman. He wished, in accordance with the ancient law, to take his brothers' widow for a wife so that he might have that pleasure before he died.

To her own dying day, she didn't know what had made her consent. Too weak to stand, the groom sat under the wedding canopy. In the bridal chamber, which was decorated with a single sprig of myrtle, she had to help him undress. She did it tenderly, caressing his wasted body as if sponging it to ease its fever. He discharged himself in her quickly and fell asleep with a happy smile.

It was the most selfless act she had ever performed. If there was a world-to-come, which she doubted, it alone would assure her a place in it.

She left the village shortly after the funeral. A few people came to say goodbye. The last was the youngest brother. Once bounced by her on her knees, he was now a broad-shouldered boy of sixteen. Of all his brothers, he resembled her fourth husband the most. She threw her arms around him and kissed him. His strong young body sprang back at her.

"Come with me to Athens," she whispered.

She slept with him for the first time in her cabin aboard ship. The sea was rough. It tossed them back and forth as if making love to them both.

She told him not to be afraid. Unlike her husbands, her lovers did not die. The lawyer from the Pelopponese was doing well. So was the teacher of rhetoric.

He didn't know what a lover was. She had to explain it to him.

They lived together in Athens for many years. People talked. She didn't mind. She was used to being talked about. Sometimes, his stiff member driving inside her while he sucked at her breasts, sucking and sucking as if he hadn't nursed enough as an infant, she felt she must have given birth to him. She at last had a child of her own.

He was a capable young man. Soon he was running the business. He expanded it, adding to the Scythian beaver furs Egyptian linens, Italian wines, spices from Arabia, copper from Spain. They now owned a large shipping firm.

She had aged. She made no effort to hide it. She did not, like other women, dye her hair or wear high collars to conceal the wrinkles in her throat. Nor did she protest when the seventh brother took younger lovers. There was no need, she told him, to keep it from her. She had learned to live without illusions. Light was not stronger than darkness. Love was not stronger than death.

Her lawyers urged them to marry. It was the only way, they said, to ensure a smooth transfer of the business when she died.

The two of them discussed it. Didn't she think, he asked, that it would be wiser not to tempt the Fates?

Surely, she said, the Fates had lost interest in her long ago. If they had once been jealous of her beauty, they no longer had the slightest cause to be.

He patted her hand. She mustn't say that, he said. Her eyes were still the envy of every woman in Athens.

The wedding was modest. Not long afterwards, one of their ships sank off Crete with him aboard.

She lived to be very old. Toward the end, her mind grew

muddled. She confused her seven husbands, calling one by the name of another. Sometimes she thought there had been only one of them. He came to her in her dreams, shy, contrite, hungry, laughing, moody, blissful, capable. She was always sorry to awake.

6

Not well did he answer them, Mellie. Not well did he answer,
saying:

> Do ye not then err, because ye know not the scriptures,
> neither the power of God? For when they shall rise from
> the dead, they neither marry, nor are given in marriage, but
> are as the angels which are in heaven.

Would not the power of God be greater could they rise as
they once were? Would it not be greater did they not have to rise
as eunuchs?

Would it not be greater could they have all they longed for:
the sound of rain falling, the taste of water from a well, the dusky
pungency of fig trees, nights dizzy with stars, the love of a
woman?

Would it not be greater if she could choose whom she loved
most?

7

At the reception for me at the Bradmans', you drank too many daiquiris. When the guests got up to go, you remained seated.

"What's the matter?" I asked.

"I can't get up," you said.

"Why not?"

"I'm not sure where my legs are," you said.

I told you, quite unnecessarily, to stay put and asked Jill Bradman to make you some strong coffee. Jill was understanding. She should have been. It was she who had kept refilling your glass from the pitcher on the table.

All the senior faculty were there: John Bradman, and Ken Conlan, and Stanimir Stankovich with Alyssia. Maximillian and Sophia Radom came, too. Radom had retired from teaching and spent all his time with his medieval Greek manuscripts, but he was still a revered figure in the department; it was he, I suspected, who had pushed hardest for my appointment. When he raised your hand to his lips while declaring his enchantment at meeting the charming wife of a promising young scholar, you had to hold back a giggle. He was, though (as we later found out) a converted Jew, the last of the Polish nobility.

The junior staff was there, too: Hal Samuelson, who I knew from Columbia, and Hugh Simons, and Joel Zakkariades, who died a few years later, and Dave Tanner and Dan Ray and Ian Rogers. Ian had just come back from his dig in Sicily and was telling us about it. From there the talk passed to the Sicilian adventures of Plato; to the university's PLATO computer project, its main headline grabber in those days; to the military–industrial complex on campus; and to the previous spring's anti-big-business recruitment riots, which we had missed by a few months.

That was when Neville Elliven spoke up. Tall and sinisterly good-looking, he had been chatting quietly in a corner with a pudgy, beak-nosed man. Now, turning to the rest of us, he observed that the rioters should have been shot.

"But Nevvy," the pudgy man said, "what would you have done with all those corpses?" He spoke with a heavy German accent.

"Sold them to a Jewish rag dealer," Elliven said.

A loud fart couldn't have silenced the room any faster. It took a moment for Jill Bradman to collect herself and whisk you and Estelle Samuelson off to see the patchwork quilt she had bought while John asked Stanimir Stankovich how his book on Diogenes Laertius was progressing.

The two men in the corner went back to chatting. They were like some macabre Abbot and Costello comedy team.

"Who was that awful man?" you asked, sipping your coffee. It was the first sign it was taking effect.

"That was the Great Palindrome," said John Bradman.

"Let him pull that in my house again," Jill Bradman said, "and I'll cut his balls off."

"The great who?" you asked.

"Try spelling Neville P. Elliven backwards," said Bradman.

"P is for Prick," Jill said.

"I can't spell it forwards," you said.

"Every department has its scandal," said Bradman. "Ours is Nevvy Elliven. He was a charter member of the John Birch Society until he resigned because he thought it was soft on Communists. Not that he isn't a good scholar – or was before he decided to save us from the barbarians. He's done some fine work on Tacitus."

"He's a fucking nut," Jill Bradman said. "And Rheingold Vogel is another. Do you know the only time he spoke to me today was to tell me my refrigerator rum cake was too sweet?"

"Jill," John Bradman said, "he's just a fifty-year-old bachelor who misses his mother's cooking."

"He's a fat little German Jew whose best friend in the department is a raving anti-Semite."

"What happened to Rita Conlan?" Bradman asked.

"She called to say she wasn't feeling well," Jill said. "Honest to God, when I saw Ken walk in with that package, I thought he was going to go off to the bathroom and come back as the Venus de Milo."

"He was only returning some books," said John Bradman.

"Why the Venus de Milo?" I asked.

"Ken likes to lecture in costume," John said. "The students love it. He draws such crowds that they've moved his class to Foellinger Auditorium. He once did the Oresteia dressed as Clytemnestra."

The Bradmans walked us to the door. You got as far as the swing seat on the porch and sat down again.

"Come on, Mellie," I said. "The car's out in the street."

"I can't believe it," you said. "A hand-kissing Pole, a bona fide Nazi, his Jewish sidekick Rheingold, and a performing drag artist — Hoo, what have we gotten ourselves into?"

We both liked Jill Bradman, though.

*

It was actually a good department. Although Elliven had published nothing but rantings for years, Vogel was first-rate. He had had a solid training in rabbinics when young and was able, though more of a medievalist, to move comfortably between classical scholarship and *jüdische Wissenschaft*. And while neither Conlan nor Bradman produced much of note, Radom and Stankovich were formidable. A few years later, they were joined by Steven Arnold, who wrote Latin poetry said not even to have been read by the judges who awarded it prizes, a bad English novel, and an excellent study of the classical epic tradition. Every day at noon sharp you could see him crossing the campus on his way to mass at the Catholic chapel.

I had an office in Lincoln Hall, where I taught beginning and intermediate Greek; my third course, Classics in Translation, was in Davenport. In good weather, I walked or biked to campus from our house on Hessel Boulevard – a rundown, dirty white clapboard cottage. The first floor had a kitchen, dining room, and living room, the second, three bedrooms. We slept in one and made another my study. The third, to be shared with a baby, was your workroom.

We settled in quickly and never more than provisionally. No matter how often we moved things around, they couldn't regain their old harmony. The small house was too big for them; they had been together for so long that they sulked when separated and resented the intrusion of newcomers – the Danish-modern couch from JCPenney, the two brass-handled oak chests we bought at a garage sale, the drop-leaf dining room table for ten. Your Navaho rug ended up by the front door, far from the round table at whose foot it had lain, which was carried upstairs to keep the loom you had ordered company. Without them, the three crows on the living room wall looked so gloomy that we banished them to the basement. Old furnishings called longingly from their rooms. The arthritic cracking of the floorboards at night could have been the sound of them searching for each other.

The house was too big for us, too. We were used to sharing a single space: a turn of the head, an outstretched arm, and there you were. Now, if I had something to tell you, I had to go looking for you. When you needed help in the kitchen, you shouted for me to come downstairs. Sometimes I bounded down gladly. Sometimes I felt torn from my work.

The front yard was neglected. We pruned its two plane trees. We bought a gardening book and garden tools, spread fertilizer on the lawn, and planted bulbs. We hoed the ground, and worked in compost and bone meal, and decided what to put where: the low hyacinths and snowdrops in front, the peonies, lilies, and daffodils further back, the tall dahlias and gladiolas in the rear. When the flowers came up, you said, they would look like the kneeling, sitting, and standing rows in a group photo.

You were for following directions. I had no patience for them. If a bulb was to be planted three times deeper than its height, you went to get a measuring tape. I took a whack with the hoe and stuck it in.

"Hoo," you said. "That's not nine inches."

"So it's seven," I said. "That's close enough."

"If you were teaching arithmetic instead of Greek," you said, "you wouldn't say three times three is seven was close enough."

We followed the pets column in the *News-Gazette*. There were Irish setters for sale in Mahomet. We were the first to get there and had the pick of the litter. Advised to take the largest pup, you chose the one that licked your nose and called him Hold Fast. That was from Henry the Fifth. For oaths are straws, men's faiths are wafer-cakes, and Hold Fast is the only dog, my duck.

We drove all the way to Springfield for a Dalmatian. I named her Baby Ruth. She had bad breath and an ignoble character. Scolded for peeing on the floor, she would stand shivering with anxiety by the puddle she had made before hiding between my legs and peeing again. We were constantly tripping over her. Dalmatians were carriage dogs, bred to run in front of horses.

Hold Fast adored you. Whenever you came home, he ran around you in so many delirious circles that I had to grab him to make him stop. As he grew older, this meant getting down on the ground and pinning him, a whirling mass of fleecy copper, into submission. By then he was regularly running away to roam the streets of Champaign. Every few days we picked him up at the pound in Bondville like a child after piano lessons.

Piano lessons would have been cheaper. We tried tying him in the yard. He howled and you ran out and freed him. After that we kept him in the house and took him on long walks, risking a summons by letting him off the leash. I sometimes let him come with me to campus and snuck him into my classes, where he lay yawning by the blackboard, the only one of my students permitted to sleep. While he never learned any Greek, he had a high IQ. One night you were reading in the easy chair with Baby Ruth snuggled next to you. Hold Fast tried climbing up beside her, but there wasn't any room and he lay on the floor regarding her jealously. All at once, he dashed to the front door and began to bark. I went to see which of our neighbors it was, Baby Ruth bounding ahead of me. The minute she jumped from the chair, Hold Fast turned around and sprang into it. Naturally, there was no one at the door.

We never got to know our neighbors well. They were friendly in that small-town way that only seems insincere if you make too much of it. They smiled when they greeted us with their gingersnap cookies and brownies on the day we moved in and they smiled the same smile when we moved out five years later. Yet why change a smile that, like the lawns in front of their houses, said what they meant it to say?

It's unique, the American lawn. Everywhere else in the world, a house is protected by a wall, fence, or hedge. The need for privacy must be close to universal. Only in a town like Champaign-Urbana would anyone walling in a lawn have been suspected of criminal intentions. Its green welcome mat declared its owner's innocence. It gave proof of his civic virtue. It proclaimed that he feared no one – that he had nothing to hide – that his hand was held out to all. And in fact, had we knocked on any of our neighbors' doors in the middle of the night to tell them we had an emergency and our car wouldn't start, they would have given us the keys to their own without hesitation.

But the lawns that hid nothing revealed nothing. Nothing happened on them. No one sat on them reading a newspaper. No one put out a card table. No one had a drink with a friend, talked to a husband or wife, sunbathed on a blanket. All anyone did was mow and rake the grass. When we had our barbecue lunches on our lawn with our friends – the Samuelsons, and Daisuke and Riko Tashahimi with their baby, and the Andrews with their two kids, and the Esterhazys, and the Millers, Shiu-Fei and Stan – and played boules or pitched horseshoes while the dogs frolicked with the children, Hessel Boulevard sniffed with disapproval. We had broken a rule that no one had realized existed. It was as if instead of smiling back when introduced to the couple next-door, we had done a cartwheel and a somersault.

Those lunches were polymorphous. They might start with your gazpacho and Riko's Japanese dumplings, proceed to steaks and hamburgers with Shiu-Fei's hot Chinese noodles, Estelle Samuelson's potato kugel, and Bill Andrews' home-made baked beans, and end with Irene Esterhazy's crepes suzettes and my thrice-boiled Turkish coffee. Everyone had something to say. Daisuke was working on the first generative grammar of Japanese. Bill Andrews was in dark matter theory. Irene taught French lit and hosted a reading group in Proust's *À la recherche* that you belonged to for a year. Stan Miller was writing a book on Zen death-bed poems. Shiu-Fei, whom he met while on a Fullbright in Taipei, was a talented calligrapher.

Still, there was something a little desperate about it all. Perhaps it's always that way in small places. You can't help wondering how your friendships would stand up to greater choice. You're like the passengers on a ship who gravitate to the same table because they find each other's company less objectionable than anyone else's. There's always the sense of having been thrown together by circumstance.

None of us intended to stay in Champaign-Urbana for long. We had our sights set higher. We had gone to graduate school in the sixties, when the academic world was awash in funds. The fellowships, the scholarships, the research grants, the appointments – it never occurred to any of us that the fount of plenty would dry up. At first, hearing of a position offered someone at Yale or Stanford, MIT or Cal Tech, we rejoiced unreservedly in a good fortune that seemed a bright portent of our own. It took a while to realize that the bright times were over.

A new decade had set in. Budgets were being slashed, departments cut back. Soon we were fighting to keep the envy from our voices when congratulating the rare colleague who had landed a job at a top East or West Coast university. Our applications were answered by regretful notes from departmental secretaries. We struggled to publish, fretted over student ratings. Even tenure at Illinois had become cruelly competitive. We worried less about being marooned there and more about being exiled still further into the great American interior. When Dave Tanner took a tenured job at a small but decent liberal arts college in Wisconsin, no one understood what he was doing. A year or two later, we all agreed he had made a wise move. It was better than Wabash or Southern Methodist.

The U. of I. looked good by comparison. It may have been a jock-and-frat school at which the Ohio State game mattered more than the history of Western philosophy and Greek life meant Kappa Alpha Psi and Delta Chi, but it was easy to keep away from all that. The jocks didn't sign up for my classes, in which there were always a few good students. I concentrated on them and gave the others their C-plus's and B-minuses at the end of the term.

It wasn't the cultural wasteland we had imagined. A lot went on. There was the School of Music, which gave wonderful concerts. There was the Krannert Center. It brought the New York City Center Ballet and Alvin Nikolai and Merce Cunningham, and Jacqueline du Prè and Yo-Yo Ma and Jordi Savall. We saw *Uncle Vanya* and *The Magic Flute* there. There were movies at the Virginia and the Orpheum and foreign films at the old Art Theater. There were decent restaurants like Katsinas and the Sea Merchant. There were even clubs on North First Street, in the black ghetto, where you could listen to good jazz and blues. You didn't have to go to Chicago for any of it.

★

Your loom arrived crated. We unpacked it and carried it in pieces to your workroom. "Hoo," you said, watching me struggle to fit two parts together, "there are instructions."

"I already looked at them," I said. "They were written by a Martian who studied English by correspondence course."

We managed to assemble it. The wood was a sunny maple. Its high uprights and solid crossbeams looked like the drawerless frame of an old secretary desk. The names of its parts, the beater, and the shedder, and the heddle, and the lamms, came from an age of shepherds' staffs and spinning wheels.

The yarn you had ordered was delivered in a large carton. You opened it and said:

"Oh, my."

You took out the balls of yarn and placed them around you in a widening circle. You knelt in the middle of them, letting their lead coils run through your fingers. You said:

"What fabulous grays!"

I had never thought gray could be fabulous.

"This one's a chenille," you said. "It's fuzzy, like fog. This is ombred. It goes from light to dark like a thundercloud."

The first thing you decided to make was a scarf for me. I said I never wore scarves. You said I had never been through an Illinois winter.

I watched you string the warp. You chose different colors of looped mohair: orange, blue, purple, and magenta. You measured the warp bouts on the warping board and wound them on the pegs and chained them and put them on the lease sticks.

"I hope I remember how to do this," you said.

You carried the warp to the loom. You tied it to the front beam and unchained it, then guided it through the heddle with the threading hook and passed it through the reed dents to the apron rod. You took it off the front beam and had me hold it, keeping the tension, while you wound it on the back beam.

You chose a forest green for the filling. You threaded the shuttle and sat on the stool with your feet on the treadles like a pianist about to give her first concert.

"Here goes," you said.

You pressed a treadle. The heddle raised the warp. You passed the shuttle through the shed, released the treadle, and passed the shuttle back. You lowered the beater, battening the filling into place.

"I'm weaving!" you said.

The shuttle went from left to right and right to left. "When the Greeks took the alphabet from the Phoenicians," I said, "that's how they wrote. They had a word for it."

"What?" you asked.

"Boustrophedon. It means 'ox-turning.' The ox plows a strip down the field, then turns and plows back up again."

You finished the scarf and took it off the loom. It shimmered like the throat of a dove.

"It's beautiful," I said.

"Boustrophedous," you said.

"You're boustrophedous."

"You are," you said. "You're more boustrophedous than I am."

Apart from one bad ice storm, that first winter was mild. Although there were blustery days, the wind blew in only one direction at a time. It wasn't like New York, where it stayed in your face no matter how many corners you turned.

There were days with no wind at all. The air was cold glass against our cheeks. If we didn't fog it with our breaths, we could see for miles. We put the dogs in the car and drove to the lake in Mahomet or to Allerton Park. With the leaves gone from the trees, the great American plains lay unveiled. Baby Ruth trotted by our side. Hold Fast dashed off to retrieve the balls we threw him, keeping them from bouncing all the way to the Rockies.

I wore my scarf every day. Returning from campus, I hung it

on the clothes tree and shouted hello. Intent on your loom, you didn't always answer.

I went upstairs. The door to your workroom was open. The dogs were sleeping on the Navaho rug.

"How's it going?" I asked.

You were working on a hammock. The warp ran the width of the loom. On the wall, you had taped a sheet of oak tag on which you had blocked out the colors in crayon.

You let out a breath. "Phwuuhh," you said.

It was your first attempt at slit tapestry. The unvarying warp was a backing for a filling that kept changing. You started and ended the filling where you wanted, knotting it to keep it in place. The slit was formed where the shuttle turned back with one color and started out again with another.

It was like painting in yarn. You were trying to shade a rose-colored strip into a black one. You wanted to merge them along a ragged line and were having trouble doing it. You had ripped them out and redone them three times.

The crayons on the oak tag were the colors of a dawn sky. "Stick with it," I said. "It will be a work of art."

"I just want it to be a hammock," you said.

*

Sometimes, watching you at the loom, I saw your glance stray to the corner of the room that we had set aside for a cradle.

I tried being cheerful about it. "There's this sperm of mine," I said, "that any egg of yours will fall in love with. We just have to introduce him to one of them."

"Why him?" you said. "Half your sperm cells are girls."

But the irresistible sperm remained shy and you went to see a doctor, who told you to keep a temperature chart. You should take your temperature, he said, as soon as you opened your eyes in the morning, before doing anything else.

You kept a chart with a thermometer by your side of the bed. One morning I woke to find your leg thrown over mine. You smelled warm and sweet. I kissed your lips. You murmured something in your sleep. I licked your breast. You shivered and turned toward me and I rolled on top of you. You woke and said:

"Wait. My temperature."

"It's all right," I said. "You haven't opened your eyes yet."

You made love with them shut. We were laughing too hard for real passion.

Somebody new — somebody who existed by virtue of not existing — had entered our lives. We lived in decimals, climbing up and down the stairs of a single degree. In the first half of the month, you hovered around 97. After ovulation, you sometimes shot up to 98.

We had to make love then. It didn't matter if we felt like it. It didn't even matter if we weren't talking, like the time we quarreled when I tracked mud on the living-room floor. Instead of ending quickly, it got worse and worse. We lay in bed all night without touching. In the morning you said:

"Oh, Christ!"

"What?"

"I'm up six-tenths of a degree."

I was already getting dressed.

"Come back to bed."

"*Now?*"

"Now."

It was awful. I tried thinking of how I loved you, of the child I wanted you to have. It didn't help. You were so desperate you took my prick in your mouth. That was something we never did.

We finished the job and I got up and dressed like a man leaving a whore.

But the worst of it I never told you.

Around puberty, I masturbated a lot. I did it lying on my stomach while imagining I was fucking some woman. It could be anyone: the maid who cleaned our apartment, the mother of a school friend, a movie actress. I had a photo of Jane Russell sitting against a bale of hay with her legs spread, breasts spilling from a dress half torn off her by an invisible assailant. One hand defended her crotch; the fingers of the other pointed toward it. Her face was hard and determined. "All right, you bastard," it said. "Let's see what you're made of." I must have torn the rest of that dress off a hundred times.

When I came in you then, Mellie, that was who I came in. Afterwards, I prayed you wouldn't conceive. In the Middle Ages men believed in succubi, beautiful demons who came to them in their dreams and bore them children from their seed. I was afraid we might have a demon child.

We didn't. Your temperature dropped. You didn't have to tell me when it did. You just put the thermometer back in its case without a word. I learned to leave you alone on those days.

We went to see a specialist in Chicago, Dr. De Michaelis. She had an office on Randolph Street. We put the dogs in a kennel and booked a room at the Allegro Hotel, toward the middle of your cycle, as we were told to do.

Our first appointment was for five p.m. The waiting room was crowded. The receptionist said we wouldn't get to see the doctor before seven and we decided to go for a walk.

We walked down Randolph to the lakeshore. The breeze from the lake was cold but not biting. It seemed to promise that winter was nearly over, that just a bit more patience was needed to see it through.

"It looks like half the women in Illinois can't get pregnant," I said.

"You only say that," you said, "because you don't notice all the ones who can."

"You do?"

"Of course. I can tell from a stomach that looks flat to you. I can tell from a smile."

"What kind of smile?"

"A smile."

I took your hand. You said:

"A few days ago I was shopping at Eisner's. Two women with babies were talking to each other in the aisle. They were blocking it and I pushed one of them aside. I didn't even say 'Excuse me.'"

"It was they who were being rude."

"No. They were just talking. I felt. . . I felt that I hated them. It scared me to feel that way."

We turned and headed back. I said:

"They don't have what we have."

"I know," you said. "But I want what they have."

"So do I."

"It's not the same."

"Why?"

"You're a man."

"A man can want children, too."

"It's different."

"Why?"

"Because you don't want them the way I do. You like the idea of being a father. It gives you pleasure to think of me nursing or lullabying a baby at your side. But it's my breasts that will shrivel if they don't nurse. It's my throat the lullabies are trapped in. Every part of me is a reproach."

Dr. De Michaelis had a nice manner. She made you feel she had unlimited time for you, which made up for her having had it for everyone before you.

"Good," she said after taking our medical histories and a cervical smear. "Your chart looks fine, Mellie. Your mucus is clear and stretchy, which means you should be ovulating within forty-eight hours. We'll try to find out what the problem is."

That called for a sperm sample and a sperm–mucus compatibility test. You would go on taking your temperature, we would wait for you to ovulate before having intercourse, and you would come back for another smear. "We'll see how many sperm cells are alive and how motile they are," Dr. De Michaelis said. "That will give us a better picture."

A medical assistant handed me a paper cup with a numbered label and pointed me to the bathroom. I had no idea how to go about it. I had never masturbated sitting or standing in my life. The minutes went by and I got nowhere. It was like kneading a lump of dough with one hand while trying to operate a broken coffee machine with the other.

There was a knock on the door.

"Someone's in here," I called.

"It's me," you said. "What's taking so long?"

"A mechanical problem," I said.

"Just do it," you said.

A minute later you knocked again.

"What's happening?"

"I'm doing it."

"Where are you?"

"On the floor," I said. "My head's under the sink." Just then I ejaculated. I rose and placed the crushed cup on the cover of the toilet seat. I washed, tucked in my shirt, zipped and belted my pants, and rattled the door handle.

"Try releasing the catch," you said.

The door opened.

"Are you okay?" you asked.

"No," I said. "How am I going to give this to anyone?" The cup looked retrieved from a wastepaper basket.

"Just leave it on the desk," you said.

I left it there. Outside on Randolph Street, the air was damp and soft.

"I'm hungry," you said.

I couldn't even think of eating.

"A good steak will get your sperm count back up."

You took me to a place called Gene & Georgetti's. You knew it from your college days. It had been a men's club then; women weren't allowed without an escort. Your boyfriend liked taking you there. "It was his way of showing off," you said. "The maître d's all knew his father and they knew him, too. We'd walk in and it would be, 'Hello, Mr. Goodman,' 'Good to see you, Mr. Goodman,' 'Right this way, Mr. Goodman.' Once we were put at a table next to Frank Sinatra."

"Good old Ed Goodman," I said.

"Al. Alan Goodman. He's probably married with four kids by now."

"And still dreaming of you."

"Not Al. He only dreamed of what was possible. He was a very practical type. That's what I liked about him. I never had to worry about anything when I was with him. He knew what to order in a restaurant, and what wine to drink it with, and how much to tip the waiter and the coat-check girl. Not like some of the klutzes I went out with before him."

"Mellie," I asked, "am I a klutz?"

"No," you said. "You're a love."

"But I am a bit of one, aren't I? I mean I can't even jerk off in a bathroom. I can't open a bathroom door."

"That's true," you said. "If it weren't for me, you'd still be in there."

The waiters were all male, just as you remembered them. They reminded me of the waiters in the old kosher delicatessens in New York, the ones who said when you asked for the roast beef sandwich, "Take the corned beef, it's better." You ordered a porterhouse and I ordered a T-bone and a bottle of cabernet sauvignon. There were signed photos of celebrities on the walls and red leather chairs instead of stools at the bar. The steaks were good. I dowsed mine with Worcestershire sauce. You let the waiter grind pepper on yours.

"Do you feel better now?" you asked.

"Yes," I said. "I mean no. I feel humiliated."

"By what?"

"By having to masturbate."

You didn't see what was humiliating about that.

"It is."

"Why?"

"Because. . . . Look, when I was thirteen or fourteen, I did it all the time. I shut the door to my room and lay on my bed and whacked off, and then I took off my sticky underpants and shoved them as far as I could into the laundry hamper and hoped the maid wouldn't notice them. One day I sat up with all that goo on me and said, 'Enough.' It was hard to stop. It was an addiction I had to break. I swore I'd never go back to it."

"My God," you said. "You sound like a Catholic priest."

"Catholicism isn't wrong about everything."

"You can't be saying this," you said. "You think masturbation is a sin?"

"Yes."

You put down your fork and stared at me.

"I'm not talking theology," I said. "I'm talking psychology."

You drank some wine. We were both on our second glass.

"When you masturbate, you're all-powerful. Every woman is yours for the asking. You can fuck her, rape her, do what you want with her, and it feels like you're actually doing it. That's what makes it addictive. It's not the physical pleasure or release. It's the power. And that only lasts a few seconds. Before the last drop is out of you, you're again a poor schmuck no woman will look at."

"That doesn't make it a sin."

"It's the sin of solipsism. That's the ultimate sin against the holy ghost."

"You are a priest. You think sex between a man and a woman is so holy?"

"I think it can be. I think it's the closest to holiness we'll ever come."

"That's theology."

"Have it your way."

We finished our steaks. "Well," you said, "I hope for your sake you don't have to do it again."

"Why would I?"

"We might have to try artifical insemination."

"You mean with a syringe?"

142

"They sometimes use catheters."

"I'm not sure I could go through with that," I said.

"What do you mean?"

"I might not want such a baby."

"Because of some ridiculous childhood guilt over masturbation?"

"I don't have any guilt. I have an intellectual and moral position. But that's not it."

"What is?"

"The baby."

"What about it?"

"I want a child who comes into the world the way children do. I want to sow my seed in you."

"That's very biblical," you said. "But you might not have enough seed or my mucus might not agree with it."

"I'd have to think about it."

"Why?"

"Because. Who knows what a sperm that starts life in a catheter might grow up to be like?"

"A solipsistic monster."

"Exactly."

"That's absurd. It doesn't know where it is. It's only for a few minutes or hours anyway."

"A lot can happen in a few hours."

"A lot could happen to you and me if you made an issue of it," you said.

We skipped dessert and walked back to our hotel. The next morning your temperature stayed low. It only rose the morning after that.

We had time in Chicago. We walked in the Loop, and saw a Giacometti exhibit at the Art Institute, and took a boat tour on the river, which wound between skyscrapers as if cutting through great rock formations. You took me to the university and showed me the dorm you lived in. You hadn't been back in ten years and were dismayed by all the modern new buildings. "You can't turn your back on anyone for a second," you said.

We checked out of the hotel and went to see Dr. De Michaelis. All the test results were excellent, she said. My sperm concentration was better than average. The motility was good. So were the morphology and pH.

Your mucus graded high, too. It ferned perfectly. My sperm was alive and well in it.

That meant we still didn't know what the problem was. The next step, Dr. De Michaelis said, was a hysteroscopy. She would fill your uterus with fluid and insert a tiny camera called an endoscope to film the uterine lining. No anesthesia was needed and she would do it in her office.

We made an appointment for it.

*

As we were leaving Gene & Georgetti's, a woman in a group waiting for a table said to me:

"I like your scarf."

I pointed at you. "That's the scarf maker."

"It's gorgeous," she said. "Where do you sell them?"

You said you didn't. You had never sold anything.

"Never?" But you should. She would love to see your work.

She took down our phone number and gave us her card. Meg Dillian, L'Atelier, an arts and crafts shop in Old Town.

A few days later, she phoned. She was driving down to see a potter she knew in Decatur and thought she might drop by.

"What will I show her?" you asked. Your entire collection consisted of three scarves, one for yourself and one a present for Irene Esterhazy; a woven tie for me; some cushion covers for our couch, and the hammock you had just finished.

"Show her the hammock," I said.

Meg Dillian loved it. "It's like a Rothko," she said.

It was almost spring, a bad time for stocking scarves but a good one for hammocks. Could you make her five more, each a little different from the others? Customers liked to think they were getting something unique.

"Five?" you asked. It had taken you weeks to make this one.

For a start. She was sure she could sell more. She would try pricing them at two-hundred-and-fifty dollars and let you have half of that.

"Mellie can't afford to make something like this for one-hun-dred-twenty-five dollars," I said. "The wool alone would cost twenty-five."

"Hoo, stay out of this," you said.

I left you to yourselves. You settled on one-fifty. Meg gave you an advance and you promised to bring five hammocks to Chicago in a month.

"How are you going to do that?" I asked.

"By knowing what I'm doing," you said. "The first time I didn't."

You made five hammocks in a month. You finished the last one the day before we left for Chicago. Someone at the College of Fine and Applied Arts showed you how to string the support ropes. It was done with cups and rings like a magic trick. We took the hammocks out to the yard and hung them on hooks I screwed into the plane trees, and I swung in each to make sure it held me. It was the end of March and a light snow was falling, but quality control was quality control.

We packed the hammocks in plastic bags and put them in the car trunk.

"Hats off," I said. "You've turned pro."

★

I sat in the waiting room while Dr. De Michaelis did the hysteroscopy. She watched it on a screen as she performed it. We spent the night at the Allegro and came back the next day for the results.

They were bad. She had gone over the photographs and consulted a colleague, confirming her first impression. You had extensive uterine adhesions. That was why you hadn't gotten pregnant.

She explained it to us. Adhesions were a scarring of the basal layer of the endometrium, the part of the uterine lining not shed during menstruation. They were generally caused by botched D&C's. A fertilized egg couldn't implant itself in scar tissue; the more of it there was, the less room there was for a placenta. She opened a book to an illustration and placed beside it a slide from your hysteroscopy. "A normal uterus is a healthy pink," she said. "You can see how yours is mostly white. That's the scarring. It's from your abortion, Mellie. Yours is far from the first such case I've seen. I could scream when I think of all the malpractitioners who are responsible."

You sat there dumbly, as if listening to a life sentence. It was I who had to ask if there was any appeal.

Dr. De Michaelis shut the book. Many adhesions were treatable, she said. There was a procedure for removing them. In your case, though, she wouldn't recommend it. The damage was too widespread and the danger of further scarring, even at the hands of a skilled surgeon, was great. That could eliminate whatever chance you still had of conceiving.

"Then there is a chance?" I asked.

"No experienced doctor would say there isn't," Dr. De Michaelis said. "In medicine, you learn to expect the unexpected. If I were you, I'd take a year off from all this. Forget about temperature charts, forget about doctors, and just enjoy life. Nature sometimes does its best when left alone. If after a year nothing has changed, you might want to consider adopting."

She hugged you when she came around from behind her desk to wish you luck.

We drove back to Champaign-Urbana. All across the flat prairie, you didn't say a word. You said nothing until we got home. Then you slammed your bag on the kitchen table and said:

"Why? Why didn't you?"

"Didn't what?"

"Let me have the baby I begged to have."

"You couldn't have had it," I said. "You know that."

"Why not? All we had to do was drive back to New York in the morning."

"And then what?"

"I would have had it. You would have married me."

"You were living with Ricky."

"Ricky and I were already finished. You married me half a year later."

"Half a year later we were lovers."

"We could have become lovers that night."

"You didn't want to."

"You didn't want me to have my baby."

"No one kept you from having it," I said. "It was your decision."

147

"It was not."

I tried putting my arm around you. "Don't touch me," you said.

"Look. I know this is terrible for you," I said. "But Dr. De Michaelis thinks there's still a chance. Let's be hopeful."

"Dr. De Michaelis knows there's no chance. Only you would believe her. Didn't you see that picture of my uterus? It looked strip-mined."

"Mellie—"

"I'm barren. I'm a barren woman. Don't you understand that?"

You lay your head on the table and wept.

I put my hand on yours. "Don't touch me," you said.

I said, "I was only thinking of you. What would you have done with a baby? The doctor had a good reputation. Cindy said he was the best."

"You were thinking of your own stupid pride. You didn't want to be the father of Ricky's bastard. You said so."

"I did not."

"That's just what you said."

"It isn't."

"It is. You said you'd marry me some other time."

"That's not fair. Who came to who and said they wanted an abortion? We sat in the Red Chimney."

"I begged for its life. We would have had more children together. Now we won't have any."

"Dr. De Michaelis—"

"It was your revenge for that summer."

"That's a crazy thing to say."

"You wanted the doctor to plow my womb and sow it with salt."

"Mellie!"

"Sow it with salt, doctor! If that's what it takes to kill her bastard baby, sow it with salt!"

It was still dark when I came downstairs in the morning. You were asleep in your clothes on the couch with Hold Fast in your arms.

8

We spent June and part of July in Paris. I had a research grant at the Centre Léon-Robin. Both Radom and Stankovich knew the center's director, Pierre-Maxime Schuhl, and helped me to get it. It was a pure perk. I didn't need to be in Paris for what I was working on, an article on Philoponus' *Against Proclus' "On The Eternity of the World"* that I later published in *The Classical Journal*, and I didn't work on it very hard while we were there.

We found a couple to exchange homes with. The husband was a mathematician involved in the PLATO project. They had an apartment in Montmartre, on Place Jean-Baptiste Clément. We took the Porte de la Chappelle line to Abbesses and walked up the hill on rue Ravignan, past rue des Trois Frères. There was a little square on the way that always had a few *clochards*, amiable souls who bowed gravely whenever we helped them to finance a bottle of wine. They made begging a dignified profession.

It was my second time in Paris. The first was after my graduation from Harvard, the summer after breaking up with Robin. I took a night train from Florence and arrived at the Gare de Bercy on a gray, foggy morning, the kind Paris wore like a shawl against the dawn chill. I had rented a room in the Cité Universitaire, and I went over to a gendarme, map in hand, and asked in my best college French *si c'est possible d'y aller á pied*. He looked at the bulging backpack I was bent under, let out a French raspberry, and said, "*Mais monsieur, tout est possible.*"

Tout est possible! I was twenty-one years old and had just driven away a girl who loved me more than I deserved, and in those weeks in Paris nothing seemed possible at all. I had never been so alone in my life, and my loneliness, which struck me as fit punishment, had a lacerating sweetness. Most fitting of all, I had fallen in love with a city that would never love me back, whose cruel beauty cared nothing for me.

I walked great distances, as if hoping to make an impression nonetheless. Each day I took a different route, sometimes up rue Bobillot to Place d'Italie before deciding which direction to head in, sometimes following the streets to Montparnasse. Once I walked all the way to Porte de Clignancourt and back, my legs like heavy suitcases by the end of the day. I talked to no one except an occasional whore on rue St. Denis and the *clochards* along the quays of the Seine. At lunchtime I sat a decent distance from them so as not to flaunt my abundance, laid out a baguette, a pork sausage, one hundred grams of yellow cheese, and a pocketknife on a page of *le Figaro*, and ate while reading the newspaper. Sometimes I fell asleep by the river and awoke hours later, the afternoon already half gone, feeling like a *clochard* myself. In my thoughts, we shared the same fate. By casting out Robin, I had become an outcast like them. I didn't believe I would ever again be loved by anyone I loved. Paris was just a foretoken.

"That's why you were such a miracle," I said to you.

We were standing on the terrace of Sacrè Coeur, looking out over the city. Countless destinies wove their patterns in the streets below, crossing, colliding, intertwining, mostly avoiding one another.

"Do you remember," I said, "how we met on the day of our wedding?"

"On Madison Avenue," you said. "I was on a bus and I saw you."

You touched your throat. Since the night we came back from Chicago, you had stopped wearing your *ángel de la guardia*.

"You said it was a sign we would always find each other. I think we would, even if we started from opposite ends of the universe."

The golden dome of Les Invalides stole the last light of the sun from the gray towers of Nôtre Dame.

"On some corner of the Milky Way," you said.

"Seriously."

"But that isn't serious," you said. "It's just a feeling that goes with being in love."

"You don't have it any more?"

"I do. But it can't literally be true that of all the billions of people in the world, we just happen to meet the only one who is meant for us."

"You think there are others?" I asked.

"I don't know," you said. "It's not testable."

"Maybe it's the other way around," I said. "Maybe. . ."

I had started a thought I couldn't finish.

"Our souls arranged to grow up in the same city, and to go to the same high school, and to sign up for the same creative writing class?"

"That was Plan B," I said. "Plan A was Martha's Vineyard." It's always hurtful to have a conviction thrown back at you as parody.

"With Moysh's party as a last fallback."

"You believed in souls once," I said. "You believed we made them."

"I believed in a lot of things. I believed that if I stopped being afraid of life and trusted it, it would reward me."

"It rewarded you with me," I said.

"Yes," you said. "Without you I'd be lost."

We circled the basilica. The moon rising over Place du Tertre was full.

We ate in a little restaurant on rue Lepic. You reached into your bag and placed something on your side of the table. It hopped to my side. Then it hopped into my lap.

"Happy birthday," you said.

It was a wind-up frog.

"Guk-guk," I said to it. We were thirty-three. "I'm still a month younger than you. One of these years I'll catch up."

A flower girl came over to us. She had three roses left, their long stems wrapped in aluminum foil like red-cheeked dolls some little child had dressed in silver evening gowns. I bought all three for you.

"One would have been enough, Hoo," you said.

"*Pour toi*," I said, "*c'est trois fois rien.*"

We went back to the apartment and put the roses in a vase. While you were in the bathroom, I took them from it, peeled their petals one by one, and scattered them on the sheet. I opened the curtain to let the full moon in.

You came out of the bathroom and gave a little gasp. I pulled you down onto the rose petals.

"Happy birthday," I said.

You had rose petals in your hair. You had a rose petal on your lips when I kissed them. Rose petals clung to your moist pubic hair when I laid my head on it to catch my breath.

★

We sat looking at the State of Illinois application forms. "Are you sure you want to go ahead with it?" you asked.

"We've been through this a dozen times," I said. "You know how I feel. It's you who needs to be sure."

"I don't know how you feel," you said. "All you've ever said is, 'If you want to adopt a child, I'm with you.' You've never said, '*I* want to adopt a child.'"

"I want you to be happy," I said. "I could be happy just with you."

"You haven't tried convincing me that I could be happy just with you."

"Because I don't want the responsibility," I said. "You blame me for not having children. I don't want also to be blamed for not adopting them."

"You'd rather blame me for adopting."

"I'd never do that. What scares me is that I might blame the child."

"For what?"

"For not being mine. For not being able to say if it disappoints me, 'Well, you made it, it's your fault.'"

"It would be your fault for having been a bad parent."

"I'm afraid I might be one. It's an instinct to raise your own child. It's not one to raise someone else's."

"It's an instinct to nurture."

"We can nurture each other," I said. "Having children is a gift. Not having them could be one, too."

"Tell me about it. I love gifts."

"Not if you're going to talk like that."

"I'm sorry. I'm listening."

"We're still lovers, Mellie. We excite each other like lovers, and we hurt each other like lovers, and we make up like lovers.

How many couples who have been married as long as we have can say that? And how often do they survive being Mommy and Daddy? Look at the Andrews. They're a great family. But Sue and Bill don't look at each other the way we do. They don't touch each other the way we do. They're hooked up to a larger circuit. Maybe we're being offered an exchange. A sadness for a happiness. Life could be telling us, 'Here's your chance.'"

"We could tell life, 'Thanks for nothing,'" you said.

We filled out the forms and returned them. An agency social worker came for a house visit. She asked us about ourselves, our health, our marriage, our finances, the baby we hoped to get.

I let you answer that. "We'd like it to be as newborn as possible," you said. "And not too obviously not our own."

"You mean white?" asked the social worker.

"Yes," you said.

"You realize that can mean a long wait."

We realized. If we were willing to take a ghetto baby or a Vietnamese war orphan, we could go to the front of the line.

"You still have time to decide," the social worker said. "I'd advise you to think about it. It's natural to want a week-old baby with your skin color, but I can assure you you'll bond just as well with an older child or one from a different background. You needn't worry it will know or understand it's adopted. Today we're in favor of early disclosure. We think it's healthier."

After she had left, I said to you:

"She was like a store owner pushing a slow item. 'Can I interest you in today's specials? We have a South Side preemie with parents in junior high school and a six-year-old of mixed

Polish-Panamanian, junky-alcoholic extraction. All you need is a valid credit card.'"

"Hoo! Don't be disgusting."

"She could have spared us the lecture about bonding. We're not tubes of glue."

"She was doing her job."

"I know," I said. "I just hate all this bureaucracy."

"No one likes it. Everyone would rather have a foundling left on their doorstep."

"Maybe she's right," I said. "We could adopt a black or yellow baby and get it over with."

"You don't mean that."

"Why don't I? We would have no illusions, it would have no illusions, and we could bond away to our heart's content."

"I wish you'd shut up," you said.

The training sessions we had to attend were in Springfield. I still remember most of our group. There was a farmer and his wife from Platt County, a couple from Peoria, and a pharmacist married to a woman from Yugoslavia. The women embraced each other warmly. The men were embarrassed and hung back. Each coped in his way. The farmer was politely withdrawn. The man from Peoria told pointless stories. He told one when the pharmacist's wife expressed her worry that she might feel no love for her baby when she got it. Our group leader said, "We're all programmed to respond to a helpless baby. That's human nature."

She had us joins hands in a circle, shut our eyes, and sway back and forth while imagining we were a cradle with a baby in it. "We'll rock it to sleep," she said. "If you let yourselves flow with your feelings, you'll be amazed how strong they are."

"I'm already amazed," I whispered to you. "They're so strong I could puke."

We shut our eyes and swayed while she sang "Rock-A-Bye Baby". Then we each said what we felt. I said:

"As a cradle, all I could think of was falling when the wind stopped."

No one laughed. You were furious. "Why don't you save your sense of humor for someone who appreciates it?" you said on our way home. "Now you'll be down in our file as a disassociating passive-aggressive."

"I'm passive-aggressive?" I said. "Maybe you can tell me why America's favorite lullaby is about babies falling out of trees. We should have been asked to imagine we were a fireman's net."

Was that the last time I made you giggle? More likely, it's only the last time I remember.

*

From Majid Fakhry's *A History of Islamic Philosophy*:

Hoo,
    I can't find Hold Fast. I'm going to look for him.

                                 m.

You came back an hour later without him.

"How did he get out?" I asked.

"The front door was open when I came home," you said. "You didn't lock it."

"I shut it. I knew you'd be back soon."

"It was open."

"Look," I said, "this isn't the first time. Either he'll come back by himself or they'll call from the pound."

Our phone number was on Hold Fast's collar. But

the pound didn't call and he still wasn't back the next morning.

"I'm going to the pound," you said. "The collar might have fallen off."

I went with you. It was a ten minute drive to Bondville. The dogs ran barking to the front of their cage as if hoping to fool us into thinking they were Hold Fast. None was.

We posted notices with a photograph. People called. Someone had seen an Irish setter running loose in south Urbana. Someone had seen one in Monticello. Someone saw a red dog along Route 10 near Weldon.

"Let's go to Weldon," you said. We had already checked out the other places.

"That's twenty miles from here," I said. "They weren't even sure it was a setter."

You already had your coat on. "I'm going," you said.

We drove up and down Route 10. We talked to people in Weldon and posted notices.

It went on like that for weeks. You drove after stray dogs you saw in the distance. You followed people walking setters on leashes. You thought you heard Hold Fast bark in the middle of the night. He wasn't at the door. "I'm going out to look for him," you said.

"Come back to bed," I said. "You dreamed it."

You dressed and went out. I had fallen asleep again when you came back. "I heard him," you said. "I'm sure of it."

"We've got to stop this," I said. "It's lunacy."

"You can stop it," you said. "I'm going to find him."

"No, you're not," I said. "If he wasn't run over, he was stolen. He could be hundreds of miles from here."

"Dogs come home from hundreds of miles," you said. "They come home from thousands."

158

"Once in a blue moon. You'll go crazy if you wait for it to happen."

"I already am crazy. Why did you leave the door open?"

"I didn't. You can't mourn him forever. He's only a dog."

"Don't you say that!" you said. "Don't you dare. It was only a baby, too."

"You can't—"

"You had to leave the door open, didn't you? You had to leave the goddamn door open."

Baby Ruth lay miserably beneath the table. A month or two later, she was killed. We were walking alongside a bridle path in Allerton Park. She ran in front of a horse, slipped on a wet patch, and was trampled.

We carried her home and buried her in the yard. We were both secretly glad to be rid of her.

★

The summer of 1972 we were in Deer Isle.

We took our time getting there, keeping off the interstates and toll roads. America still wasn't all shopping malls. There were drugstores with soda fountains and gas stations where someone worked the pump. We spent a day in Amish country, visited an old college roommate of yours in Glen Falls, and wasted most of a morning looking for the commune in Vermont where Cindy Moses was supposed to be living. We finally found it at the end of a dirt road the turn-off to which we missed twice. There were some shacks and tents, a rusting tractor, a poorly weeded vegetable garden, and a shitting goat tied to a tree. Most of the men had long hair; some of the women were topless and the smaller children ran around naked. It was like driving into a native encampment in the

Amazon. Cindy had left the previous winter, no one knew for where.

You were taking a month-long workshop in figurative tapestry at the Haystack School. It was given by an elderly Scotsman who had studied when young with a disciple of William Morris and you were one of ten applicants accepted.

We rented a bed and breakfast in a house overlooking Southeast Harbor. There were rocks descending to the water, down which we could climb if we were careful not to slip on the sea-moss. The gulls circled and dived for clams along the shore. They soared with them in their beaks, dropped them on the rocks to split them open, and swooped down to claim their prize. When they had eaten their fill, they flew out to the bay and took a seat on the water. At rest on the waves, they looked like gray lobster buoys.

Your workshop met every day. I rented a bike and explored. One day I saw a sign on a waterfront shack that said, BOAT RENTALS & SAILING LESSONS. A man cutting squid for bait inside the shack said he charged twenty-five dollars a lesson. Five of them, he thought, would be enough. I asked when we could start and he said, "How about now?"

And so ἱστὸν δ' εἰλάτινον κοίλης ἔντοσθε μεσόδμης στῆσαν ἀείραντες, we raised the mast of fir and stepped it in its socket, and κατὰ δὲ προτόνοισιν ἔδησαν, ἕλκον δ' ἱστία λευκὰ, we made fast the forestays and hoisted the white sail. It bellied out in the wind – ἔπρησεν δ' ἄνεμος μέσον ἱστίον – and the dark waves sang loudly past the boat's keel and she skimmed them quickly, accomplishing her way.

Apart from the aluminum mast, it was just as Homer described it. We weren't twenty yards from shore when I felt something like joy. The wind, the spray in my face, the roll and rush of water beneath me: it was almost like the first time we made love.

The wind! "Tell me where it's coming from," said my mentor. We were still standing on the shore, at the head of a narrow inlet, with a small, rocky island about half a mile away.

I wet a finger and held it in the air.

"You can use that to wipe your ass with," he said. "Where'd you learn that, in the Boy Scouts?"

"I was never in the Boy Scouts," I said.

"Shut your eyes."

I shut my eyes.

"Face into the wind and feel it on both ears. You feel it?"

"Yes."

"Now turn your head all the way to the right."

The wind was only on my left ear.

"Now all the way to the left."

It was only on my right ear.

"Good. Get it on both ears again."

"Got it," I said.

"Now turn just a little to the left. Where's it stronger?"

"On my right ear."

"The other way. Now?"

"On my left ear."

"Move your head back and forth until it's the same on both."

I did. "It's about the same," I said.

"I didn't say about."

I moved my head some more. "It's the same."

"Open your eyes. What are you looking at?"

"That tree past the tip of the island."

"That's where your wind is," he said. "It doesn't matter if it's an itty-bitty breeze or a gale. A sailor can tell you where the wind is faster than he can tell you his own name."

Since then, Mellie, I always know where the wind is. Not just if it's blowing in my face or not, but where it is.

When I came for my fifth lesson I was told, "Take her out by yourself today. Stay this side of the island and watch out for rocks."

I took the boat out and brought it back safely. The next time I sailed it past the island and around the point. By the time I persuaded you to join me on a weekend, I had sailed all the way to Oceanville.

At first you were afraid. There was a stiff breeze and the boat heeled. "Are you sure this won't turn over?" you asked.

"Yes," I said. "There's a manufacturer's guarantee."

After a while you relaxed. It was a cool, sunny day. Globules of sunlight hung on the waves. "This is lovely," you said. "It's like riding a horse. We're galloping on water."

"Did I ever tell you about the time I took riding lessons?" I asked.

"No," you said.

"It was the summer I waited on tables in the Catskills."

"After your first year at Harvard."

"My second. Another waiter talked me into it. I didn't like it from the start. The horses scared me. I just didn't want to admit it and quit. The first time we went out on a trail, my horse broke into a gallop. I pulled on the reins but couldn't control him. Suddenly I heard the riding teacher shout behind me, 'Fall! Fall!', so I let go of the reins and jumped. He rode up to me and said, 'What are you, crazy? Who jumps from a galloping horse?' I said, 'You told me to.' He said, 'What do you mean?' I said, 'You shouted, "Fall! Fall!"' He said, 'You idiot! I shouted "Pull! Pull!"'

"Poor Hoo," you said. "The mad stunt rider of the Catskills."

"I was lucky I only cracked a rib. A boat's a horse you can trust."

We had reached the entrance to Southeast Harbor. Penobscot Bay lay ahead of us.

"We'd better head back," you said. "I need to put in some time at the loom."

You were working on a tapestry of the Maine coast that you wanted to finish before the workshop ended.

"Do you know that the Greek word for sail, *histion*, also means a weaving?" I said.

You said, "Sails must have been woven. How else could they have been made?"

"They must have been," I said. "But that isn't the reason. That's that *histos* meant both a mast and the beam of a loom."

We tacked and headed back. I gave you the tiller and let you steer until we neared the dock.

Your workshop ended with a party. The tapestries were hung on the walls. Yours was all dark greens and grays: dark trees and gray rocks and gray water. If there had been a sky in it, it would have been dark and gray, too. It looked even darker next to Art Sunderland's hot-rodders working on a bright red convertible. Art came from West Virginia. He played the banjo and said "gosh" and "darn," and his and yours were the two best things done at the workshop.

There was a clambake with music and dancing. We stood on the edge of it, watching. "Let's dance," I said.

You shook your head.

163

"Come on," I said. We hadn't danced in years.

You danced for a while and stopped.

"What is it?" I asked.

"I can't," you said. "It's not in me any more."

I said, "Let's take a walk."

We walked through the woods to the water. The tide was out. On the rocks lay bulbous-headed stems of kelp washed up by the waves. They looked in the starlight like dark, luminescent leeks. The waves beat against the rocks wearily.

"Don't be sad," I said.

You stared at the waves. We hadn't heard from the adoption agency since having been placed on a waiting list.

"I've been thinking," I said. "Maybe we should go away somewhere."

"We are away somewhere."

"Further. I could ask for a leave of absence next year."

"You can't, Hoo. You'll be up for tenure soon. It's no time to be away."

"Fuck tenure."

"That's easy to say."

I chucked some kelp into the water.

"Where would we go?"

"I don't know. Maybe to a Greek island. It wouldn't cost much to rent a house. Once the summer crowds are gone, the islands are empty."

"What would we do on an empty island?"

"You'd weave. I'd write. I might try writing a novel."

"I didn't know you wanted to write one."

"You're talking to a former editor of *Helicon*."

"God," you said. "We're twice the age we were then."

"We'll have a sailboat. And dogs that can run free."

"No dogs," you said. "I couldn't stand any more heartbreak."

"A boat with our own little beach. On winter nights we'll drink ouzo and listen to it storm."

"That sounds nice," you said.

The sounds of the party reached us through the woods.

You rose from the rock we'd been sitting on. "Shit, I'm all wet," you said. "We'd better go say our goodbyes. We still have to pack."

We made it back in two days, driving ten hours a day. We picked up the New York Thruway at Albany, took the Ohio Pike and the Indiana Toll Road all the way to Gary, and then cut down and across.

★

The telephone rang at ten-thirty. We were in bed, reading. "Who the hell is that?" I asked.

You picked up the receiver. "Yes, it is," you said.

"No," you said. "It's all right."

"Yes, we do," you said.

I put down my book.

"Tomorrow?" you said.

You made a scribbling motion on your palm. I got out of bed and brought you a pen and paper.

"Yes," you said. "Where?"

"Who is it?" I whispered.

You shook me off with an impatient gesture.

"Yes," you said. "Yes.... 74 to Galesburg.... Where?... No, just the last part.... The first traffic light, yes.... Right... How do you spell that?...You'd better give me a number."

You wrote it all down

"We'll be there," you said. You hung up.

"We'll be where?" I asked. "Who was that?"

"The social worker," you said. "They have a baby for us."

I stared at you.

"It's in a hospital in Galesburg. It was born four days ago."

"Holy shit," I said.

"We have to pick it up tomorrow morning."

"Tomorrow?"

"That's what she said."

"Why did they wait to tell us?"

"I don't know," you said. "Maybe someone ahead of us dropped out at the last minute."

"It's in Galesburg?"

"Yes."

"That's the other side of the state."

"We'll leave early. Oh, my God, Hoo. We're totally unprepared. We don't have baby clothes. We don't have diapers. We don't have bottles or formula."

"I'll buy everything tomorrow," I said. "You'll give me a list."

"We'll have to clear out the corner of my workroom. There are cartons of yarn there."

"I'll do it now."

"Don't bother. We don't have a cradle."

"Why didn't they at least give us a day's notice?"

"She didn't say. What time is it?"

"A quarter to eleven."

"It's too late to call Sue. Do you think it's too late to call Sue?"

"Probably. I'll have to cancel my classes. What do you want Sue for?"

"I need to talk to her. I don't know what to do with a baby. I don't remember a thing from our training sessions."

"There's nothing to remember. They were a waste of time."

"Do you think it's too late?"

"I think we should go to sleep," I said. "We have a long day ahead of us."

I set the alarm and turned out the light.

We lay taking a walk in the darkness. I could never tell from your breathing if you were asleep or not. The only sure sign that you were was the little tremors that broke out in your hand. It was as if the last, leftover energy of the day had been waiting for a chance to slip off and join the entropy of the universe.

I held your still hand in mine. "What are you thinking?" I asked.

"Nothing," you said. "Crazy thoughts."

"Like what?"

"Crazy thoughts. I was thinking the father might have murdered the mother and escaped, and they have to place the baby in a hurry before he comes back and murders it too."

"For craziness, that's not bad."

"Suppose something's wrong with it."

"What could be wrong?"

"It could be a Down's baby. That's why the couple ahead of us didn't want it."

"She'd have told you."

"She didn't want to tell me anything. She sounded stressed. It could have been born with the cord around its neck. There could be brain damage they don't want us to know about."

"They'd never hide that."

"They might suspect a genetic disease."

"Go to sleep."

"Hold me."

I held you tight.

"I should have called Sue," you said. "I've never even diapered a baby."

"Sue couldn't have told you how to diaper a baby over the phone. We'll call her from the hospital. She'll come over as soon as we get back."

"What if it won't drink from a bottle?"

"Why shouldn't it?"

"There are babies that only want the breast. They won't suck a rubber nipple. It could dehydrate before we get home."

"It hasn't dehydrated in the hospital."

"I hoped they checked it for jaundice."

"Calm down," I said. "It's the baby you wanted. Feel happy."

"I can't. I'm too nervous."

You got out of bed.

"Where are you going?"

"To pee."

You came back and I spooned you. I dreamed I was at a reception at the White House. President Nixon was there. I had something to tell him that could save him from impeachment, but he kept being approached by other people and I couldn't get his attention.

"Are you sleeping?" you asked.

"I was," I said. "You just woke me."

"I can't sleep. What time is it?"

I pressed the button that lit the clock. "Almost one."

"I can't stop thinking."

"About what?"

"We don't have a baby blanket. What will we wrap it in?"

"We'll use a bath towel."

"I'll have to sit in the back with it."

"That's fine," I said. "It's too young to drive anyway."

"I just thought of something."

"What?"

"We don't have a baby seat."

"You'll hold it in your arms. I'll drive carefully."

"What if a policeman stops us?"

"Go to sleep."

"I can't."

I dreamed a policeman asked me for my high school diploma. I searched in my wallet and couldn't find it.

"Are you sleeping?" you asked.

"I was dreaming that I never graduated from high school."

"I haven't slept a wink. What time is it?"

"Two-thirty."

"Hoo?"

"What?"

"How can we live on a Greek island with a baby?"

"Why can't we? The Greeks do it."

"That's different. They have big families. They're all related. In a crisis everyone helps out."

"We'll make friends."

"How? You can't speak modern Greek. You'll tell them the baby needs a doctor and they'll think you're asking for some olive oil."

"As far as I know, the word for doctor is still *iatros*. It doesn't have to be next year. I haven't applied for a leave of absence yet."

"We might have to put it off for several years."

"That's even better. By then I'll have tenure. We can go without worrying about it."

"I thought you didn't care about tenure."

"I wasn't a father then."

"What time is it?"

"Twenty to three."

"I have to go to the bathroom," you said. "I've been peeing all night."

"It's just tension."

You flushed the toilet and got back into bed.

"Hoo?"

"What?"

"Maybe we shouldn't adopt it."

"Why not?"

"Suppose it's the wrong thing to do."

"It's the right thing. We decided that long ago."

"I know. But I didn't think I'd react like this. I'm in a panic."

"You'll get over it. A normal mother has nine months to get used to the idea of having a baby. You haven't had nine hours. It's natural."

"It's not natural. The whole thing isn't natural. A woman I don't know had sex with a man I don't know and went around with a fetus inside her, and tomorrow it's going to be mine. I don't feel anything a mother should."

"You will."

"What if I don't? What if all I can think of is that another woman felt my child kicking in her belly and has the milk it's screaming for?"

"You'll get over it."

"Suppose I don't."

"That's adoption, Mellie. It's what you wanted."

"What *I* wanted. Not what you did."

"What I did, too."

"No, you didn't. You're doing it for me. You said so."

"We're in this together."

"You put it all on me."

"Now I'm to blame again."

"I'm not blaming you. I'm in a panic, can't you see?"

"Breathe deeply."

"I feel I'm having a heart attack."

"The only heart attack will be mine if I have to drive to Galesburg and back on no sleep. Everything will be fine, I promise. Just relax."

"What time is it?"

"Almost three-thirty."

When the alarm went off, you weren't in bed. A smell of coffee came from downstairs. You were sitting at the kitchen table.

"Is there any coffee left?" I asked.

"No," you said. "I'll make more."

"I'll make it," I said. "Go shower. You should freshen up before we go."

You said, "We're not going."

"What do you mean?"

"I'm calling the hospital."

I sat down across from you.

"We're not adopting a baby," you said.

"This baby?"

"Any baby."

"How—"

"I've made up my mind, Hoo."

"But that *is* crazy. For the past three years you've gone

171

around in a depression. Now you're getting the child you were depressed over not having – and you're giving it up because of one bad night?"

"It wasn't just a bad night. A twenty-foot python was coiled around me and squeezing."

"Is it still?"

"No. I'm fine now. I was fine the minute I realized it wasn't too late. I'll call the hospital soon. I have their number."

"Why don't you just tell them we can't make it today? Say our car broke down or something. We need to think about it when we're not groggy from a sleepless night."

"There's nothing to think about. I'm not too groggy to know I don't want to be a mother just to sit in a playground watching my child throw sand at other children. I thought I did. I thought I wanted all that. But that was just because I couldn't have what I did want. I wanted a child to grow inside me. I wanted to push it out into the world. I wanted it to look like you. That would have made me so proud."

"You can be proud of raising the child you adopt."

"No, Hoo. That's what last night was about. I'm not made to rescue homeless babies. I'm like you. If we didn't make it, I don't want it."

"We won't have another chance," I said. "No adoption agency will look at us after this. We'd never have the strength to go through it all again anyway."

"I don't want another chance. Do you remember what you said to me in Paris? Let's take the gift, Hoo. Let's be lovers. Let's be lovers all our lives."

"You won't hold it against me?"

"No."

"Do you swear?"

"Yes."

"Okay," I said. "Let's go back to bed."

"You go," you said. "I'll stay up for a while and call the hospital."

I woke to find you sleeping beside me. I jumped out of bed, had a quick breakfast, and barely made it to my eleven o'clock class in time.

9

Should I have insisted we take a day to think it over? What difference would that have made? You had made up your mind. I wouldn't have fought to make you change it. At heart, I was relieved.

And so the Cimmerian years began, ἠέρι καὶ νεφέλη κεκαλυμμένοι, and grievous night spread over unhappy mortals. We didn't know it at first, just as no one knew the Dark Ages had set in when Rome was sacked by Alaric. Night fell slowly, as it falls on summer days in northern, Cimmerian lands. What would we have longed for, Mellie, on our Greek island? The patient drip of summer rain, mouths profligate with berries, the cool translucence of long twilights in which there always is time for one last game of hide-and-seek.

That last game of hide-and-seek, do you remember? It was at last getting dark. All things were losing their color, and this time, running for the trees at the end of the lawn while the child who was It counted to a hundred, you were entering a dimness as thick as the forests of fairy tales in which one always got lost or met a witch. You almost wished you would be the first to be tapped and taken prisoner, tap, tap, Mellie, behind the tree, chained to the safety of the just-switched-on porch light of the bungalow in which the moths circled in flurries, trapped in a vortex they couldn't escape.

But the child who was It stuck too close to base to see you. The bright-leafed maple that had laughed with the jays all day long now spoke in the somber tones of the fir tree by the front door. Base sticker, base sticker, the hiders called tauntingly, like night birds hooting in the dark. Yet one by one they were caught, tap, tap, behind the bush, and tap, tap beneath the swing, and tap, tap against the wall, until only you were left. The deck chairs on the lawn were crouching lions and now was the time to dash past them and free all the prisoners, but the distance was too great. And so you stayed where you were, waiting for the game to end, come out, come out, the call would come, come out, wherever you are. But no call came, and fireflies winked in the grass, and the front door opened and shut and there was silence, and the new fear gripped you that you had been forgotten.

Do you remember, Mellie?

I didn't apply for a leave of absence. Stankovich, who had taken over as department chairman, urged me not to. My chances for tenure, he said, were excellent. Why spoil them? Out of sight was out of mind, and I needed a good library if I was to do research and publish. The Greek islands were not about to go away. The last one to sink was Atlantis, he said.

We took his advice and opted for a summer on Sifnos. While we were there, we would scout for our Elysian isle. A week before our flight to Athens, you came down with shingles. We canceled and lost our deposit.

The summer after that we were with the Andrews in Truro, in the house of Sue's parents who were yachting in the Caribbean, and the summer after that we stayed in Champaign-Urbana. I had reached the last chapter of my book on the late Neoplatonists and Stankovich was pressuring me to get it done and find a publisher so that it could go into my tenure portfolio.

The time in Truro was difficult. We should never have gone. Sue and Bill's children were five and seven, and everything revolved around them. They were nice, sweet kids, which only made it worse, because the child we hadn't adopted tagged after them everywhere. Sue's father kept a boat in Wellfleet and Bill and I sailed a lot. You came along once or twice and preferred after that to stay home. In the end, we made some excuse and drove back to Illinois a week earlier than planned.

We drifted away from the Andrews. We drifted away from everyone. Everyone had children. The Samuelsons had three, and the Esterhazys and the Millers one each, and Daitsuke was pregnant with her second. Our picnic lunches moved to other lawns, and all the pâtés and potato salad you made for them couldn't keep us from feeling we had come empty-handed. A mob of youngsters crawled and ran about. We alone didn't have one to chase, scold, lift, hug, or comfort.

At dinners or evenings out, children were the main subject until it was changed for our benefit by a pointed look we had to pretend not to notice. Gradually, we stopped inviting; then we stopped accepting invitations; then they stopped coming. There was no unkindness in it. Our isolation was self-imposed. Now and then, someone called to ask how we were. The phone relationships went on longer but eventually lapsed, too.

You and I never discussed our decision. Only once did it come up between us. We were guests for dinner at the Esterhazys'; the Millers were there, too. We sat down to eat late because Julia Esterhazy didn't want to go to sleep, and halfway through the first course she began to cry. Irene rose to go to her. Istvan told Irene to sit down. The cries turned to screams. Istvan restrained Irene again. Julia had to learn, he said: if she wasn't taught that good night meant good night, putting her to sleep would just get harder and harder. Irene cleared away the dishes and went to bring the main course. Julia screamed louder. We ate dutifully while she wailed like a car alarm that no one was bothering to turn off. At last she stopped. Irene went to have a look and came back grim-faced. Julia had fallen asleep against the bars of her crib with one arm reaching through them. "She looked like a prisoner shot trying to escape," Irene said to Istvan. "You didn't have to be so cruel."

Istvan said it wasn't cruel to be firm. "You'll see," he said. "The next time will be easier." "There won't be any next time," Irene said. The Millers intervened and a conversation began about parenting. For once no one was deterred by our presence. It was still going on when we went home. You said:

"If people can't put their children to sleep, they shouldn't have company."

"They didn't know Julia would have a screaming fit," I said.

"That was no reason to make us sit through it."

"To tell you the truth," I said. "I minded the screaming less than what came after it. I wish they weren't all so earnest about their children."

"What should they be?" you asked. "Flip and facetious?"

"No," I said. "Just a bit more humble. Not everything children grow up to be or do depends on their parents."

"Well," you said, "if Julia Esterhazy grows up to hate her father, you'll know why."

"Julia's loves and hates won't turn out to have been so predictable," I said. "Children aren't that easily molded. They come with their own character. They get it from ancestors we don't even know about, from beyond that. Parents are just the guardians of it all. There's a sense in which every child is adopted. Sometimes I think—"

You interrupted me. "Stop! Stop right there! I don't want to know what you think."

"But what did I say?" I asked.

"It's what you were going to say."

"If you're so sure you know what I'm going to say," I said, "I might as well not say anything."

"Then don't," you said.

I didn't. Not for the next twenty-four hours. But you were right. We had made a decision. It was treason to question it.

The Cimmerian years!

We fought often. We had sworn to stay lovers, to shut out all the rest. But it was all the rest that deflected the sting of the foolish remark, the thoughtless act, the uncalled-for criticism, the insensitive oversight. Children turned a couple into a small country with a government, a populace, laws and enforcement agencies. Its cabinet had to go on meeting even when its ministers were feuding.

We were only a couple. We had no place at the councils of state. We owned no shares in the future. Had we known that the world would come to an end in a hundred years, we might have felt less anguish than we felt at the prospect of another day of silence between us.

The nights were for repairing the days. The violence of their passion was new to us. We hurled ourselves at each other as if to shatter what had hardened and could only be smashed forcibly. Asleep, we lay wrapped around each other like poultices. Our bodies came apart with the sound of adhesive tape being unpeeled.

They were too short, the nights. We took afternoon naps, pulling off our clothes and falling asleep instantly. In winter, when darkness came early, we opened our eyes and plunged back into sleep, deluded into thinking we had more hours ahead of us. On afternoons when you had to be somewhere, or I had a class to teach, we felt deprived.

We had our routines. It had been a mistake to think life would be more spontaneous without children. The truth was the opposite. Children forced you to be flexible. You never knew when they would have to stay home with the measles, be driven to a friend's house, need help with their homework. We were more creatures of habit than most people. We had less patience for interruptions or distractions. Although much of our time was ours to do with as we liked, we liked most to do what we did yesterday.

I had my work. You had yours. You were getting a reputation. Meg Dillian wasn't happy about it, but you were now selling in New York. The summer I stayed home to finish my book, you were invited to assist at a workshop in Haystack. It was the longest we had been apart. I wrote telling you how I missed you. You wrote telling me how you missed me.

My book was accepted by Princeton University Press. I was given tenure. You took me out for dinner and we ordered champagne. You insisted on paying with your credit card. "Why don't we go halves?" I asked.

"Absolutely not," you said. "This is my treat. You worked hard for it."

We laughed. We had a single joint bank account.

Our Greek island was on hold again. It made sense to put it off. Three years of being an assistant professor would entitle me to a partial sabbatical on full salary. Added to my summer vacation, that would give us half a year at the university's expense. Meanwhile, I thought we should buy a house. My pay was going up and we could afford a mortgage.

You weren't keen on it. "Why do we need to own a house?" you asked. "We're fine where we are."

I said it was a wise move financially. It was no different from renting, except that you wound up with property.

"I know that," you said.

"Then why not do it?"

"How long can we go on living here?" you asked.

"Until I get an offer from someplace better," I said. "I thought we agreed it wasn't so bad here."

"It hasn't been. And I can put up with it for a few more years if I have to. But buying a house is. . . ."

"What?"

You looked down at your hands. You still wore your jade ring, on the finger next to your wedding ring.

"It's a good investment," I said.

"Hoo," you said, "do you remember the princess? From the bus station in Philadelphia?"

"She left the castle and crossed the moat," I said. "That was the last I heard of her."

"Would you like to know what happened to her?"

"Sure."

"Then listen," you said. "She wandered all day in the mountains and fields, keeping off the roads, because she knew the king her father would send out search parties. Toward evening she reached a town she had seen many times from her window. She was so bruised by the thorns and brambles she had fought her way past that no one could have guessed she was a princess. She was hungry, thirsty, and tired, and wondering what to do next, she absent-mindedly touched the ring on her finger. Just then she saw a sign on an inn that said: 'Chambermaid Wanted.' She knocked on the door, and despite her appearance, which she explained by saying she was a country girl who had gotten lost on her way to the city, her good manners so impressed the innkeeper that he hired her and gave her a little alcove to sleep in.

180

"The next morning the princess went to work. At first her clumsiness nearly gave her away, because she had never made a bed or folded laundry in her life. But she learned quickly and became skilled at her job. One day she was polishing cutlery in the dining room when she noticed two young men at a table. They were glancing at her while whispering. Finally, they came over. They were pilgrims, they said. They were setting out on their way to…where did people go on pilgrimages in those days?"

"Which days?" I asked.

"The days of castles and princesses."

"Medieval pilgrimages? God knows. Rome. Compostela. Jerusalem."

"Some place like that. They were setting out for it. The princess asked them what a pilgrim was. The young men had trouble explaining it. They could only say they could see she was one, too.

"'How do you know?' the princess asked.

"The young men said they knew because all pilgrims recognized each other.

"The princess wanted to know how. The young men shrugged. Pilgrims could do that, they said. That was the sign they were pilgrims.

"The princess wasn't sure she understood it very well, but she knew she couldn't stay in the town much longer without being discovered and returned to the castle, and so she asked the two young men if she could join them.

"The young men were delighted. First, though, they told her, they would all have to take three oaths.

"The princess asked what these were.

"The first oath, they said, was always to remain true to each other. The second was never to turn back from their journey. The third was to tell no one they were pilgrims. Any pilgrim met on the way would know who they were without being told.

"And so they took the oaths and set out, wandering together from place to place. Now and then they fell in with other young people and traveled with them. Such times were jolly. But although the princess studied these companions closely, none struck her as a pilgrim, nor did any appear to think she was. Sometimes she wondered if the two young men hadn't made it all up.

"One of them was a student. The other was a vagabond. The princess was very fond of them both. There were times when she thought she loved the student more than the vagabond and times when she thought she loved the vagabond more than the student. She had never lost her heart to anyone, and now, so it seemed, she had lost it to both of them at once."

"Tell me," I said. "This vagabond. What did he look like?"

"He was very good-looking," you said. "He had beautiful, rich dark hair, and pale skin, and a fine, thin nose before it was broken in a brawl."

"I was just curious," I said. "Go on."

"You can probably guess what happened next. In their travels, they came to a deserted barn outside a town and decided to spend the night there. The student went into town to look for food. The princess and the vagabond lay down in the hay to rest. Before they knew it, they were embracing. It didn't occur to the princess that she was breaking her oath to the student. Had he been the one beside her, she would have given herself to him just as gladly. If only she and the vagabond hadn't fallen asleep! The student returned, found them entwined in the hay, and vanished without waking them.

"The princess and the vagabond were now alone. They had been a threesome for so long that it felt strange to be only two. That didn't last long, though, because they soon came to a large port. The vagabond wished to continue by sea. The princess didn't. They argued, and the vagabond boarded a ship and sailed away.

"The princess was left by herself, penniless in the great city. I won't tell you about all she went through while she was there. Although she often thought of selling her ring, each time she remembered the moth's warning. She made many friends but recognized no pilgrims among them. She never forgot her three oaths. Yet she had no idea if the vagabond and student remembered them too, or where they were, or if she might not now be the only pilgrim in the world."

The champagne was making me sleepy. "Why don't you get to the end?" I said.

"There is no end yet," you said.

"Then to wherever the story is up to."

"I'll make it short. The princess met the vagabond and the student again. She married the student and the vagabond died. She and the student reached a village in which they stopped to break their journey. That was years ago. They're still there. They're even thinking of buying a house. The princess spends her days at her loom. Sometimes she thinks of the castle and of the king and queen, but that all seems far away. Sometimes she thinks of the vagabond. She and her husband rarely talk about him."

You were looking for the end that was no end.

"The other day, the princess was thinking of how she first met the two young men. She remembered the inn – she even remembered the gleam of the cutlery when she held it up to the sunlight in the window – but she couldn't remember where the two of them were bound for. It had slipped her mind. It wasn't even on the tip of her tongue. If she took an atlas and looked at every page, she wasn't sure she could find it. Maybe it was never a real place."

"Is she still a pilgrim?" I asked.

"That's what she asked herself," you said.

★

We bought a house on Green Street, near campus. It was a 1920s, four-bedroom Craftsman Style house with a low-slung front and a set-back, snugly sloped second story, from which rose a small attic with a dormer window. The rooms were large and airy and their roof beams were exposed, making your loom, where they beveled down over it, seem part of the construction. It was in excellent condition, having belonged for many years to an engineering professor and his wife who took good care of it.

I took a bedroom for my books and put my desk in the attic above it, which was reached by a flight of steep stairs. Getting the desk up them wasn't easy. You thought it was foolish, but I had always dreamed of working in an aerie. There was just enough space for a chair, the old music stand I kept my *Oxford Universal Dictionary* on, and a shelf on which I put the wind-up toys you had given me, one for each birthday. You had had to look hard for them, because everything now ran on batteries. There were twelve: the monkey in his race car, a woodpecker on a tree, an Indian on a horse, a pink rabbit with a snare drum, the frog, a little pig, a helicopter, Captain Hook, a ladybug, a mouse, a duck, and a dwarf. Each birthday I brought them downstairs and had them perform for you. The monkey steered his car, the woodpecker pecked at his tree, the Indian reared on his horse, the rabbit brushed the snares, the pig waddled and oinked, the frog hopped, the helicopter spun its blades, Captain Hook waved an iron claw, the ladybug crawled, the mouse ran on little feet, the duck bobbed up and down, and the dwarf patted its round belly. Happy Tiger marched in front of them like a drum major leading a parade.

The Year of the Dwarf! We were nearing forty. The quotation mark on your forehead rarely faded. Yet when I think of you that day at the farmer's market in Rantoul in your Marimekko dress, your straw hat, and your sunglasses, you really did look like a princess — not one who had run away from a castle, but one who wasn't being followed by a horde of paparazzi only because they didn't know she was hiding in Illinois.

What were we doing in Rantoul? We had gone to look for a rutabaga for the Swedish casserole you wanted to make for our birthday dinner. A plain turnip wouldn't do; it had to be rutabaga. On our way back to our car, we passed an antique shop with an odd item in the window. It was a rattan piece the height of a coat rack, with a triangular frame of three poles. Each pole had a series of wooden pegs, one above the other, and each trio of pegs held a round, platter-like disk.

We couldn't guess what it was and stepped into the shop to ask. It turned out to be a nineteenth-century pie stacker. Back then, the shop owner said, housewives sometimes needed to cool and store large numbers of pies baked for festive occasions. The pie stacker was designed for that.

You loved it. You said we could put our Limoges dishes on it. But it was three-hundred-and-fifty dollars and the shop owner wouldn't come down. "They're very rare," he said. "You hardly see them any more."

I let you tell him we couldn't afford it because I had already decided to buy it for your birthday. I drove back to Rantoul the next day, paid three-hundred-and-fifty dollars, loaded it into the car, drove back with it, and carried it up to the attic.

My birthday present was the dwarf. When you went to the kitchen to bring the casserole, I ran to fetch the pie stacker. You took one look and covered your eyes as if hoping it would be gone when you took your hands away.

"What's wrong?" I asked.

"You shouldn't have," you said.

"But I did," I said.

"Well, you shouldn't have. I don't want it."

"It's a birthday present."

"I don't want it."

"Why not?"

"Because I will not have a three-hundred-and-fifty-dollar pie stacker in my house. That's half our monthly mortgage."

"It's actually a bit more," I said. "Why don't you just take it as a token of how I feel."

"I don't need your tokens," you said. "You don't have to impress me with how much you think I'm worth."

You were ruining our birthday. "Oh, Jesus, Mellie," I said. "I wasn't trying to impress you. I wanted to give you something you loved."

"That was very sweet of you," you said. "And now you can return it."

I lost my temper. "You can return it yourself," I said. "And if that's too much trouble, you can give it to charity with that two-dollar dwarf you think *I'm* worth."

I shouldn't have said that. You ran to the bedroom. I ran after you. You slammed the door.

The Year of the Dwarf!

The casserole went into the refrigerator beside the birthday cake. I returned the pie stacker. The shop owner didn't mind. It was worth more in his window than sold.

Next-door to the antique shop was a bookstore. Some books were on sale on a table on the sidewalk. One was a volume of Van Gogh reproductions. My first thought was a mean one. It was that, at the four dollars fifty it was marked down to, I had found the perfect gift for you. But I began to leaf through it and all at once there were tears in my eyes. I bought it and that night I wrote you a letter on the blank page inside the cover. I wrote:

Mellie,

I wanted to write you a love letter and this is the nicest stationary I could find – but when I bought this book in a bookstore in Rantoul, that wasn't why I bought it. I bought it because it moved me to come across Van Gogh in Rantoul, the way one is moved in a city street by a wildflower sprouting from the pavement or the call of a woodland bird. Van Gogh in Rantoul! Well, why not? But it moved me. No artist ever meant to me what he did. What he still does – because looking at this book, and especially at the paintings from those last two incredible years in Provence, I was as overwhelmed as I was on that day when we stood in front of one of them in the Museum of Modern Art. And it made me happy to know that the artist we loved has survived in me undamaged, that whatever dulling of feeling or perception I sometimes feel has taken place in me since, or whatever increment of experience or knowledge, I have carried him safely through it all, so that looking at it today, all the excruciatingly painful, joyful, life-drunk, God-drunk, suffering exaltation of his work was still intact for me. Do you remember what you said about the cypress tree? If I could learn to pray again from anyone, it would be from Van Gogh.

A love letter? But you know, there are times, moments, when my love for you overwhelms me all over again just like Van Gogh in Rantoul. It can happen unexpectedly, just thinking of you, or looking at you, or hearing your footsteps. Suddenly, it's all there, as wonderful and miraculous as it was in those first years. I think loving you is the only reason I fear growing old. I can't bear to think I might look at you one day and not find you beautiful. How will our love live in old bodies? How will it recognize us, or we it?

Not long ago I dreamed you had died. I was on Broadway. I walked into the Red Chimney and asked if anyone had seen you, but no one had, and I walked back into the street – it was a summer evening, but cool, as though after a rain – trying desperately to think where you might be, because Broadway was in the underworld and I needed to find you. How would you manage there without me? How could I leave you by yourself? But I was already waking from my dream. I did so in two stages. Only in the second was I overcome by relief that it was just a dream. The first was full of anguish that I was being taken from you, that I would have to return without you.

O my love! When did our love become a cage in which we tear and tear at each other? Still, holding this book in my hands, I know there is no hardening of emotion, no weariness of soul, that Van Gogh could not pierce instantly, that he will always be there to wipe my eyes and heart clean when they are crusted over with the soot of time.

He is something, isn't he?

Hoo

I meant to give it to you in the morning. But in the morning, I don't remember why, we quarreled again and the book remained in the attic.

*

Just before I left for that conference at the University of Texas, a strange thing happened.

Our next-door neighbor was a line technician at the Kraft Food plant. He worked the night shift and came home every morning in the dark. Or so you told me afterwards, because I was a heavy sleeper and wasn't aware of it at the time. A little after four, you would hear his car turn into the driveway, the car door slam, and his footsteps crunch on the gravel.

That winter he died of a sudden heart attack. He was what people call "tragically young," a man in his fifties. We paid a condolence call on his wife. She was in a state of confusion. The flow of callers seemed only half to convince her that her husband really was dead.

A week or two later, you were woken at night by the slam of a car door. There was a crunch of gravel. At that exact moment, you said, I began to groan in my sleep. Then I cried out in fright.

You shook me to wake me. I had been dreaming. In my dream, I was in a room with a door. All at once, the door began to open. It opened slowly and I realized that an invisible presence

189

was entering the room. I ran to the door and tried to shut it, but it went on opening with a slow, relentless force that threw me backwards on the floor.

You looked at the clock. It was a little after four.

★

Now comes the hard part.

Hard because I didn't dream it too.

Hard because there isn't a day I don't wish I did.

Hard because it would have been — as you said, Mellie, as you said – bad enough if I had simply fucked a woman at a conference.

She came up to me during the break in the morning session, after I had given my talk. "Hi," she said. 'I'm Lynn Harrison."

"I know you're Lynn Harrison," I said.

"You do?" She blushed, pleased but puzzled to be recognized.

"Yes," I said. "It's written all over you."

She looked down at her name tag and laughed. "And for a second I thought I was famous! I forgot I was wearing it. I hate these things. I wish I had the courage to go around without them like you do."

"It doesn't take much courage to be anonymous," I said.

"It does when everyone else has a name. Excuse me for taking off my glasses. They're new bifocals. I'm having trouble getting used to them."

It didn't call for an apology. Viewed without impediment, her eyes were such a clear blue that a bird might have flown right into them.

"I loved your talk," she said. "I've worked on the late Neoplatonists myself."

"Just a minute," I said. "Harrison. Didn't you publish something on Pseudo-Dyonisius in *The Modern Schoolman*?"

"Yes," she said. "Don't tell me you read it."

"I did," I said. "It was interesting."

"Interesting as in 'What's an inoffensive word I can use without having to say it was any good?'"

"Interesting as in 'I learned a lot from it.'"

"Oh." She had what appeared to be nice breasts. "Wow."

We stood facing each other. "What's the next lecture?" she asked.

I checked the program in my jacket pocket. "Henosis and Theosis in Eastern Monophysitism. Kenneth McClosky, the University of Western Ontario. Have you ever heard of him?"

"No," she said. "Have you?"

"No."

"Let's play hooky," she said. "It's a gorgeous day."

We found a place to sit on a terrace away from a path along which students came and went.

"This is a big improvement on the weather in Illinois," I said.

"Wait till you live in Idaho," she said. "It was eighteen below when I left. What shall we talk about?"

"Anything but henosis and theosis."

I had three thoughts as I said that. The first was that I was flirting. The second was that I hadn't flirted with a woman for so long that I hadn't realized I was doing it. The third was that something in me was intensely curious to plumb Lynn Harrison .

Should I have gotten up then, Mellie, and walked away? *Damn, I just remembered I have an appointment with the curator of the rare manuscripts collection at the library*? But it was already too late to still the stirring in my groin.

We talked about ourselves. Lynn grew up in South Carolina. She had had a tough childhood. Her father, a small-town lawyer, was abusive. Her mother was a semi-alcoholic. "I was pretty wild myself," she said. "By the time I was out of high school, I had done drugs and sex and everything. If today I teach at a university and have three adorable children and a wonderful husband, that's one of the minor miracles of God's creation."

"How did God pull it off?" I asked.

"With the help of a high school guidance counselor. I wasn't even thinking of college and she talked me into going to South Carolina State in Orangeburg. In my freshman year, I took a Great Books course. All I had ever read until then was *The Bobbsey Twins* and *Nancy Drew*. Suddenly I was reading Dante and Shakespeare and Milton. It blew my mind. My favorite was the *Odyssey*. I dreamed of being white-armed Nausicaa with Odysseus clasping my knees and asking if I was a mortal or a goddess. My section teacher was from the Classics department and I asked him to say that to me in Greek. He did and I said, 'That is the most beyootiful thing Ah eveh heard. Ah've got to learn that language.' That's how I became a Classics major."

"And lost your southern accent."

"Just put it in storage, honey."

"The *Odyssey*."

"Yup. It's your turn."

I talked for what must have been hours. We went to a hot dog cart and bought hot dogs and soft drinks and brought them back to where we were sitting and went on talking. We were playing hooky from the afternoon session now, too. I told her about you, about us. I said things I had never said to anyone.

"Fighting isn't everything," she said. "It sounds like the two of you still have a big love."

"We do," I said. "On the day before our wedding, I wrote Mellie a letter. I said that if I had a thousand lives to live, I'd want them all to be with her."

"*That* is a long-term commitment."

"I still feel that way. I just keep it to myself. It's like a coin I carry around in my pocket. I keep touching it to make sure it's there, and when I'm alone I take it out to look at, but as soon as I hear Mellie coming, I put it away."

"Where it's safe."

"She has a bitterness now. It's awful to see. I sometimes think we should have adopted that baby."

"You'll never know."

"We never will. She's never forgiven me for that abortion."

"It was the sensible thing to do."

"Sensible things can be foolish."

"And vice versa."

"Like what we're both thinking of doing now?"

Our legs that had touched dangled over the terrace wall. On the concrete ledge beneath us, our shadows had outgrown us.

"I won't pretend it hasn't crossed my mind."

"And it doesn't. . . . I mean, thinking about your husband?"

"Dick? Look, I take my marriage seriously. I was married when I was nineteen. I've slept with two other men in fifteen years. That doesn't make me a serial adulteress."

"I've been faithful to Mellie," I said.

"That was your mistake."

"What do you mean?"

"You've never forgiven her, either."

"For what?"

"For Ricky. That's the other pocket. The one with the hole."

"I forgave her long ago," I said.

"That's not what it sounded like. You evened the score with him. You'll forgive her when you've done it with her."

"I'm sure she'll be grateful."

"I'm not asking for her gratitude. I just don't want to make love to a man who's going to feel guilty about it."

"I'll be cheating on someone I love."

"So will I, honey. Did you ever go to summer camp?"

"No," I said.

"I did. The summer I was fourteen I was sent to Scout camp. My daddy thought it would help build my character. Mostly it built my back muscles, because I spent a lot of time with one boy or another on top of me. They were just too dumb to know what to do about it. Anyway, there was a lake in which we swam. Before we were allowed into the water, the swimming counselor divided us into couples and give each couple a number. Every few minutes he blew his whistle and you had to find your buddy and take his hand and hold it in the air. The counselor shouted 'Count off!' and each couple called 'One,' 'Two,' 'Three,' 'Four,' until everyone was accounted for. The rest of the time you could splash around all you wanted, but you had to be there with your buddy when the whistle blew. It was your job to make sure he didn't drown. That was an absolute rule. You were thrown out of the water if you broke it."

"He who hath ears, let him hear," I said.

"Amen," Lynn said.

I'm not going to describe that night again. Whatever I told you about it was true. Did I say she and I made love more than once? We made love more than once. Did I say the first time felt so strange, with everything in the wrong place, all the soft parts and the hard parts and the secret parts, that I almost had to stop? It felt so strange that I almost had to stop. Did I say that after that I enjoyed it? I enjoyed it. Did I say that once she screamed so loud that I put my hand over her mouth? I put my hand over her mouth. All those details are stupid. Most descriptions of sex are stupid. Human beings are more alike having it than doing almost anything else. What do they expect to be told that they don't know?

And besides, I remember mostly words, disembodied ones, as if whoever spoke them left them behind in the hotel room when checking out, as if they were still being spoken there:

"That was good."

"It was wonderful."

"Better than the first time."

"Yes."

"Who are you?"

"I'm the man who just made love to you."

"No. You! Who are you?"

"Stop poking me. I'm the man without a name."

"No. You! You! Who are you?"

"All right, I'll confess. Just don't poke me. I'm an immortal essence."

"Me too."

"Pleased to meet you."

"Me too."

"I loved that. I love you."

"I loved it, too."

"Do you love me?"

"I hardly know you."

"You know me better than anyone. You were just touching my guts."

"Is that where I was?"

"Say you love me."

"I love the linnet's wings. You're Lynn the linnet."

"You love me. Say it."

"I can't."

"You can. Say it."

"I love you too."

"Where's your hand?"

"Here."

"Let's do buddies."

"What?"

"That's what Dick and I call holding hands when we fall asleep."

"Oh."

"Do you and Mellie have a name for it?"

"Taking a walk."

"What are we going to do now?"

"Get out of bed and go to the conference. We can't miss the last session too. People will talk."

"I'd love to hear what they say. What are we going to do?"

"After the conference?"

"Yes."

"Go home."

"Will you tell Mellie?"

"I don't know. I don't think so."

"Call me tonight."

"Tonight?"

"Dick plays basketball on Wednesday nights. Call me at ten. The kids will be in bed."

"I'm not sure I'll be able to."

"I'll need to hear your voice."

"I'll try."

"We're Rocky Mountain time. You must be Central."

"Yes."

"Call at eleven your time. We'll meet again soon. Somewhere halfway. Maybe Denver."

"Lynn, I can't do that."

"You can't do what?"

"I can't start meeting you in all kinds of places."

"Not all kinds. A nice one."

"I can't."

"Why not?"

"I can't lead a double life."

"I'm not suggesting we meet every week. I'll take what I can get. A few times a year would be fine."

"I can't, Lynn. That's lies, and alibis, and duplicity. It's a sordid path. I'm not going down it."

"You mean this is it? You'll just walk out of here and forget me?"

"I won't forget you. But why ruin it with all that ugliness? We'd just end up hating each other."

"As one immortal essence to another, fuck you."

"You see? It's happening already."

"You're making it happen."

"Don't cry."

"Fuck you."

"I have a buddy. So do you."

"Thanks for reminding me."

"The parable was yours."

"We're not living in parables."

"It was a good one."

"All right, I'll tell you what. Give me a life."

"A life?"

"You promised Mellie a thousand. Give me one."

"How can I give you a life I promised Mellie?"

"Just one. Out of a thousand. Or is that too much for you to spare me?"

"No. It's not."

"A whole one. Just you and me."

"All right. One life."

"You'll call me tonight? Dick doesn't usually come home before ten-thirty."

"I'll try."

"Call me."

"How do I look?"

"You look fine."

"We'd better not leave together."

"You go first. I'll wait a few minutes."

"Should we sit together at the session?"

"No. We shouldn't talk during the break, either."

"Couldn't I come up to you and say, 'Hi, I'm Lynn Harrison?'"

"Not unless you want to miss your flight."

"Call me tonight. I put my number in your wallet."

"I'll try."

"Call."

"All right."

That's what I remember, Mellie. Disembodied words, as if no one were speaking them, as if they were still being spoken to this day.

My flight from Austin was routed through St. Louis. I had a two-hour wait for my connection, but fog set in and I was still on the ground five hours later. I called you and said I'd get in late. I would take a cab. You shouldn't wait up for me.

I was in a mood of strange and solemn euphoria. The blood ran tingling to the tips of me. It was as if a clot inside me had dissolved. I had never felt so expansive. I loved life. I loved Lynn. I love the lady doing the crossword puzzle next to me. It was just as Lynn had said. I had forgiven you for something I hadn't known you weren't forgiven for. From now on, everything would be different. I would be more patient, more forbearing. I would leach the bitterness back out of you. You would never know what had brought about the change in me. You would simply feel it like a change in the weather.

You surprised me by being at the airport. You ran to me and I lifted you off your feet.

"What are you doing here?" I asked.

"I missed you terribly," you said.

"I missed you, too."

"I couldn't wait to see you," you said. "I. . . . Don't be mad at me, Hoo. I didn't mean to snoop in your study. But I went up there to look for a stapler and I saw the Van Gogh book. I read your letter. Why didn't you give it to me?"

"I was going to. We had a fight."

"It was beautiful. I cried and cried."

"That must be why your eyes are so shiny."

"Yes," you said. "You wiped the soot of time from them."

We drove home from the airport. "I started work on a new tapestry," you said. "It's a secret. You'll have to keep out of my workroom until it's finished."

"If I have to, I will," I said.

199

"Don't feel hurt. You'll understand when you see it."

But it wasn't hurt that you heard. It was worry. It had just occurred to me that you would want to make love when we got home. We hadn't made it in a long time and there was now such tenderness between us. And I was drained dry. There wasn't a drop of sperm left in me.

You had hung a sign saying WELCOME HO(O)ME on the front door. It was almost eleven. I slipped away to my study and phoned Lynn. The conversation was short. She really did just want to hear my voice. Then I went to the kitchen. All I could do was take my time and hope you would fall asleep while I did. I found a bowl of leftover spaghetti in the refrigerator, emptied it into a pan, and heated it.

"Hoo, where are you?" You were calling from the bedroom.

"I'm having something to eat," I called back.

"Come soon."

I ate the spaghetti while looking at the newspapers and went to the bathroom. I took a long shower and dried myself slowly and shaved, lathering myself twice. Then I brushed my teeth and tiptoed to the bed. You were lying with your eyes shut.

I slipped into bed. "What took you so long?" you murmured. You put your arms around me and kissed me. I kissed you back without ardor. You said, "Hello, my love," and kissed me again. My prick was limp. Fear flooded my chest.

"What is it?" you asked.

"Nothing," I said. The blood was flowing back the other way now, pounding on the gates of my heart like a routed army.

"What?"

"I must be tired," I said. "I didn't sleep much last night."

"Why not?"

"I don't know. I was thinking of you."

"Well, here I am," you said.

"Yes," I said. "Here you are."

"'Hoo," you said. "Something's wrong, isn't it?"

"Nothing's wrong," I said.

You sat up in bed. "You better tell me what it is."

I told you. I told you like a suspect who breaks down at the first question asked him. I told you like a criminal convinced he can get away with his crime who comes running with the evidence to convict him. I told you like a liar whose talent for lying has deserted him all at once.

You went to the closet for a bathrobe and sat down in the chair by the bed, your face a tight mask. "How many times did you fuck her?" you asked.

I told you.

"Was it good?"

I told you.

"Was she better than I am?"

"Mellie, please."

"Was she?"

"No."

"I'm better than she is?"

"Mellie."

"Am I?"

"No one's better. It's different."

"I'll bet it is. What did you talk about when you weren't fucking her?"

"Things."

"What things?"

"Thoughts. Feelings."

"For each other?"

"That too."

"Did she say she loved you?"

"Yes."

"Did you say you loved her?"

"Not. . ."

"Did you?"

"Yes."

"You bastard."

"She made me say it."

"You lied to her?"

"I. . . . She's a special person. There are things to love about her."

"What?"

"She's a pilgrim, Mellie."

"Don't use that word."

"She has a pilgrim's soul."

"She had the hots for you, that's what she had. She saw the bulge in your pants and went for it."

"Absolutely. She was drooling all over my dick."

"Did she suck it?"

"No. She wasn't keeping a temperature chart."

"Fuck you."

"That's just what she said."

"When?"

"She wanted to talk about meeting again. I told her I couldn't. I said I was married to you, that I didn't want another woman in my life."

"What did she say?"

"Fuck you."

"What else?"

"She asked for a life with me."

"You'd just told her she couldn't have one."

"Not this one. Another. I'd mentioned that letter I wrote before our wedding. The one about living a thousand lives with you. She asked for one of them."

"What did you say?"

"I said just one."

"You *what*?"

"Just one. Out of a thousand."

"I don't believe it. You gave away a life with me?"

"For God's sake, Mellie," I said. "You never believed in that."

"It doesn't matter," you said. "It doesn't matter what I believed in. You had no right to give away what was mine."

"I'll get it back."

"How?"

"I'll call her and ask for it."

"You'll call her and ask for it! 'Lynn, my darling, you know that life I gave you? Well, it turns out that Mellie wants it back. How about exchanging it for four more fucks?' Is that what you'll say?"

"I—"

"You know what she'll say?"

"What?"

"The same thing I say. That you're a shameless son-of-a-bitch. Get out of here, Hoo. Get out of this room. Go live all the lives you want with her. I don't want to see you again. Get out!"

I took the clothes I needed for the morning – I had an early class to teach – and slept downstairs. The trial was over. Now I would wait to see what my sentence was. I never imagined it had already been pronounced.

★

From J.P. Postgate's *Gai Valerii Catulli Carmina*:

I've left. I didn't want to wait for you to come home. It's easier this way.

I took a suitcase of my things. I took a few of my books too. When I get settled somewhere, I'll come back for the rest.

It would have been bad enough if you had simply fucked a woman at a conference. We might have worked that out, though. What you did went beyond that.

You had no right.

I went upstairs to your workroom. Your loom was strung with a backing. The design was on a sheet of oak tag. Two ghostly figures walked down a moonlit corridor. Behind them, on the corridor's wall, hung an unraveled tapestry.

10

When the meltemi blows here on Sforthos, my house feels about to be hurled off the mountainside. Last night it rattled a loose iron shutter like a village of women banging pots against an eclipse. I opened the window to tighten the bolt and the wind flung a fistful of dry bougainvillea leaves in my face. It's said to have given the island its name by a metathesis of *sfodros,* wild or violent. Perhaps that's so, although it blows just as hard all over the Aegean.

We're the smallest inhabited island in the Cyclades. You won't find it on most maps. The only town, called Sforthos too, has a population of less than a thousand. That's all-year-rounders. In the summer it's more, mostly Greek families from the mainland. We don't get the bikini-and-backpack crowd. There's just one small sand beach and a few cafés and tavernas for entertainment. The big ferries out at sea, plowing their way to Paros or Naxos, are the size and shape of white rubber erasers. When summer comes, I rent my house to vacationers and move down the back slope of the mountain to an empty hut. It belongs to the Stavritises, who own the minimarket in town and let me stay in it. It has no electricity or water, but the rent helps get me through the rest of the year.

This is my third. Soon after getting my full professorship, I applied for early retirement. No one so young had done that in the history of the university and I was turned down. I reapplied, was turned down again, and applied a third time. By then the administration was glad to get rid of me. My severance pay was modest but enough.

I sold the place on Green Street at a good profit after paying back the mortgage and sent you the entire sum. I wasn't being generous. I just didn't want any part of it.

In the beginning, I expected you back soon. I told myself it would be the same day. When it wasn't, I counted on the next day. Then Sue Andrews called and asked to speak to you, and I realized you had left town without telling anyone. For a while, I kept silent, too. I went around pretending you were there, like a man hiding a corpse.

The only one to know at first was Lynn. She said she hoped it would blow over quickly. "You can tell Mellie I'm returning her life," she said. "I didn't want to wait that long to see you again anyway." She didn't suggest that we meet, though. I didn't think the only reason was her knowing I'd say no.

In the end, you called. You were staying in Glen Falls and wanted to come for your things. All you would take, you said, was your loom and your books and clothes. You would leave me everything else.

I didn't want everything else. I wanted you.

"You should have thought of that before," you said.

You refused to see me when you came. I had to promise to be out of the house. But I didn't promise not to watch from a distance and I was standing at the corner of University and Green when you pulled up with a U-Haul. You got out of the car with someone I didn't know and went inside. Then whoever it was came back and carried empty cartons into the house. When I returned to watch you leave, the U-Haul was gone.

I should have tried to get in touch with you. I should have driven to Glen Falls. But I had what you once called my stupid pride. You had made me stand in the winter street straining for a glimpse of you. I wasn't going to beg.

I got through each day. I taught my courses. I graded papers and exams. I traveled as much as I could. Anywhere was better than the house you no longer were in. In Luxor, I was reminded of you by a dance. That's practically the only thing I remember from that whole trip.

And then I heard you were living with Art Sunderland. It must have been in the early spring of the following year, because the dogwood in our yard was in bloom. Every year I had cut you a branch of it. I grabbed an ax, ran out to the yard, and chopped the tree down.

I could have killed him with the same ax. I had spent a night with another woman and you were with him every night. Every night! I tell you, I can't imagine a worse torture than lying awake in bed and thinking of you in someone else's arms. Do you know how many nights like that I've spent? Try five and one-twelfth times three hundred and sixty-five.

And why? Because of something you didn't even think was real. You must admit that has its comic side.

Or were you beginning to have doubts? The slam of a car door, the crunch of gravel: did they make you wonder?

Yet what good would it do us to be ghosts? What good would it do to be Geoffroy and Melisande, holding hands that never touch, kissing with lips that never meet?

What is a ghost but a soul looking for its body? Why else would it return only to the places they were together, as we do when we look for what we've lost?

They were wrong, Mellie: Ammonius, Plotinus, Porphyry, Iamblichus, Plutarch of Athens, Syrianus, Proclus, and all the others. They thought the soul, the wise soul, would be glad to lay down its burden. They didn't know it would be inconsolable, that it would always grieve for the legs that had carried it, the arms that did its work, the mouth that fed it, the cheeks that felt the wind.

Once we stood on a dock and kissed. The sun was warm, the water was cold. The pond trembled at your splendor. What soul basking in divine radiance could feel what we felt then? What soul would not forsake God's presence to feel it again?

What soul does not long for the resurrection that they denied, Ammonius, Plotinus, Porphyry, Iamblichus, Plutarch of Athens, Syrianus, Proclus, and all the others?

There is a discussion in Al-Ghazali entitled "On refuting the philosophers' denial of bodily resurrection and the return of spirits to bodies." As usual, he presents the philosophers' arguments at length. Since every corpse, they say, decomposes in the earth, the soul could not be restored to its original body but only to a replica of it. Moreover, even if the processes of nature were reversible and the original body could be reconstituted from its elements, it would have to reassume the last form it had and risk rising again old, ill, infirm, toothless, or even missing a limb. Outrageous paradoxes would follow. In a case of cannibalism, for instance, two souls would vie for the same body, since the cannibal's would have been nourished by its victim's.

Al-Ghazali's refutation is brief. He merely demonstrates that none of the philosophers' objections logically precludes God's ability to work a miracle. In the course of this, he mentions a strange belief. There are people, he writes, who think that at the time of the resurrection a great shower of sperm will rain down on the earth, bringing forth all the human bodies that existed. And he says: "What improbability is there for there being among the divine causes something similar to this, which we do not know, that results in the resurrection of

208

bodies and their being rendered disposed to receive their former souls?"

A bizarre image. Yet how many times, tormented at night by the thought of you, was I comforted by it? I pictured the rain falling steadily, steadily, as rain falls on gray summer days. It drips from the clouds, from the roofs, from the trees. When the sun comes out at last, each droplet hanging from a branch is a little encapsulated rainbow.

A bicycle stands against a tree. I mount it and ride off. At first the going is hard. The wet grass squishes beneath the wheels. Soon, though, I reach a paved road. Behind me is a town. I pedal quickly, joyfully, as though it were my first day on earth. The road dips and curves and I lean into it, feeling the wind. At the bottom is a bridge across a bay. I speed over it, swept by my momentum. A girl is standing there, looking down into the water. I have to brake suddenly to keep from hitting her. "Hey, watch it!" I say.

"Watch it yourself," she says.

"I could have run right into you."

"It's a good thing you didn't."

"I could have busted my bike on your braces."

She giggles. "What's your name?" she asks.

I tell her. "What's yours?"

"Mellie," she says. "That's short for Melisande."

It always stops there.

I suppose Ricky would tell me to concentrate on my breathing and let the projector run.

It's all projection, all maya. I've never thought otherwise. It's just a game of the quanta.

But they draw the wrong conclusions, the swamis and rinpoches. What were our best moments? When were we at our most intense? Wasn't it when lost in the game so completely that we forget that that's what it was? Do we really need a wise voice to remind us we're only seeing images on a screen?

The wind has died down. It will pick up again this evening. Soon, I'll walk to town to buy groceries and check the mail. It's half an hour going and longer coming back, because it's mostly uphill then. The first few hundred yards leave my property and cut through Kostos Vassilliadis' olive grove. After that starts a dirt track that passes the Vassilliadises and the Nassos, runs by a garbage dump that is the island's only eyesore, and joins the road from Sforthos to the Ayos Pantaleimon monastery. From there you descend the mountain in a series of hairpin turns, the sea first on one side, then on the other. In clear weather, you can see Paros.

The town itself isn't much. As you enter it, there's an auto repair shop, a gas station, and – facing the port across a square with a patriotic statue of Demetrios Ypsilantis – a small branch of Alpha Bank, two cafés, two restaurants, two tavernas (one of each closed in the off-season), the Panellenikos Hotel, Stavritis' mini-market, a nautical supplies shop, and a post office, mayoralty, police station, and firehouse all in one building. In the side streets going up the hill are a bakery, a butcher shop, a fish store, a greengrocer's, a pharmacy, a hardware store, a barber shop, and a newly opened video rental. Further up is the church with its blue dome and bell towers.

The port is small, too. There's a breakwater, a slip for the little ferry from Paros, a fuel pump, and a low seawall at which the boats anchor stern-to. Two or three fishermen regularly stand there. I've never seen them land a fish, but they make themselves useful by catching the mooring lines that the arriving boats toss ashore and slipping them over their bollards.

I keep my boat at the far end of the seawall. Mostly, I sail it around the island. Sometimes I beach it on the pebbly shore beneath the monastery and walk up to the top for the view, or tie it to one of the pine trees that drop to the water's edge at Vorro Akroterio. There's a grotto there where the sea rushes in and spumes up through a crevice as though through the blowhole of a whale. Once I sailed to Paros and spent the night there. I was becalmed on the way back, spent a second night at sea, and didn't do it again.

It's a quiet life. I read a lot. I read the books I read long ago, the ones I brought with me to Sforthos. Last winter I picked up *Great Expectations,* which I hadn't opened in years. A note fell out of it that said:

⌄

I'm at my parents'. My mother isn't feeling well. Call.

✘

When was that? Your mother was as healthy as a horse. I had forgotten what a master Dickens is. I had forgotten the ending. "We are friends," Pip tells Estella, who answers, "And will continue friends apart." But in the next sentence, the novel's last, Pip takes her hand and says, "The evening mists were rising now, and in all the broad expanse of tranquil light they showed to me, I saw no shadow of another parting from her."

No shadow because this time there won't be one? Or because this time they won't part?

I keep to myself. Now and then Vassiliadis looks in on me. He sends his son Manalis when something needs to be fixed, and every year I get a big tin of olive oil from him and his wife. I sometimes visit the Stavritises, and that's the extent of my social relations. In town, I'm just the American who bought the old Alexiou place. That's fine with me. I'm living the life I thought I would live, the life I imagined on the quays of the Seine.

I haven't made love to a woman since you left me. Not that there have been many opportunities, but I've spurned the ones there were. From time to time, I have erotic dreams. Sometimes you're in them. They end in frustration. We embrace and then, as our passion mounts, the telephone rings, or there's a knock on the door, and you have to go get it, leaving me to ejaculate onto an empty sheet. Once, though, you went on clinging to me and I came in you. The sweetness of that moment still remains with me.

I'm off to town now. I'll buy a few things at the minimarket and drop by the post office. The clerk will be the pretty girl with the fuzzy lip who needs to see a cosmetician. It was she who handed me the letter two months ago. It was addressed to me in a neat, looping hand. My heart raced. My first thought was that you were writing to ask for the divorce you hadn't asked for until now. I was afraid to open it. You wrote:

Hoo,

I'll be in Europe in May. I thought I might come to see you on your island toward the end of the month. Would that be all right? It would probably be around the 26th or 27th. Let me know.

Mellie

The return address was a street in Old Saybrook, Connecticut. I wrote back that I would love to see you. You answered that you'd arrive on the 24th, on the ferry from Paros. I wrote that I'd be waiting for you at the ferry slip.

No critic has ever studied a text more closely than I studied those two letters. *I'll be in Europe* – did that mean you would be traveling by yourself? Even if it didn't, *I thought I might come* meant no one else would be with you on the ferry. That didn't prove you were living alone, but it didn't prove you weren't, either. I had heard nothing about you since, a year after moving to Sforthos, I had a visit from the Millers, who told me that you and Art Sunderland were in West Virginia. Had you left him and moved to Old Saybrook? It didn't strike me as a place for a single woman. That wasn't such a good sign.

Your island. Well, naturally you knew where I was, you couldn't have sent me a letter if you didn't. Still, *your* island – didn't that sound as if you knew I'd been here for a while? If you were keeping track of me, that was a better sign.

Hoo, Mellie: at least not coldly formal.

The 24ᵗʰ. Because you couldn't wait to see me? No, that was foolish. But it couldn't have been an oversight that you didn't say how long you were planning to stay. Wouldn't that have been the normal thing to do? *I'll arrive on the 24ᵗʰ and leave on the 28ᵗʰ?* You didn't ask me to book a hotel room for you, either. Could you have done it through a travel agent?

I took a look at a nautical calendar. The moon is full on the 27ᵗʰ. You must have known that. Or not. You were going to Europe, those were the days you had available, you tacked me onto a trip you were taking anyway. If you had wanted to see me badly enough, you could have flown from the States at any time.

I'm so nervous and excited I can't think straight.

Next week you'll get off the ferry. I'll spot you at once. There still aren't that many passengers at this time of year. Will you have changed? Will I look old to you? I sometimes think I've gone from being young to being old with no transition.

I'm scared, Mellie.

We'll take a taxi to my house. I've asked a woman to tidy up and I'll stock the refrigerator. I'll show you where everything is and go to the hut. Before I do, I'll give you this book. I began it the day I received your first letter.

You'll read it. Then we'll talk. I'll only say now that if I had a thousand lives to live, I'd want them all to be with you.